HOLLER & HOWL

MOSH SERIES BOOK 1

SUSANNA ROGERS

Bucher & Reid

This is a work of fiction. Names, characters, businesses,
places, events and incidents are either the products of the
author's imagination or used in a fictitious manner. Any
resemblance to actual persons, living or dead, or actual
events is purely coincidental.

Bucher & Reid

Cover by Amygdala Book Design
978-0-6484920-7-8

ALSO BY SUSANNA ROGERS

MOSH SERIES
Holler & Howl
Down & Dirty
Slash & Burn
Light & Shade
Ride & Crash
Ground & Pound

YOUNG ADULT
Infiltration (Book 1)
Regeneration (Book 2)
Validation (Book 3)

Parallax Error

CHAPTER ONE

Lily

Walking through a doorway shouldn't have been this hard, not with two smiling bouncers who ushered me through while they checked everyone else for ID, not with Nick waiting inside the bar, but then he was the whole reason my nerves were on edge. The reason I was here.

The place had been a dump the last time we were here. No, the last time *I'd* been here. There was no 'we' anymore. And it was still a dive, only more crowded than ever because this was Nick's place now, and he knew how to party.

Easing his way through the crowd, he swaggered toward me with the confidence of a man who ruled the world. More than the bar that belonged to him. The whole town did. The prodigal son returned.

He held my gaze, his blue eyes so devastating I couldn't look away if I wanted to. My life flashed in front of me and in that instant, I was eighteen again and in his arms, and there was nowhere I'd rather be because no one made me feel the way he did. Hard to believe that was only five years ago.

How could he do that to me? How dare he? Because there were so many other moments too, moments we didn't have and wouldn't have, moments that could never be. Gone before they'd happened.

"Lily." He took my hand in his and leaned across to kiss me on the cheek, making me feel wanted and warm and secure even though none of that was possible, not with Nick. I should've hit him, pushed him away. I should've hated him.

I kissed him back demurely. If anyone looked at us, they'd never know what had been and maybe he didn't know either.

"The famous Nick Steel." I forced a smile then took a small step back to try to give myself some distance. "So this is Nick's place now?"

"Nah," he said. "It'll always be The Swamp."

I laughed. "Can't argue with that."

"We need a drink."

I swallowed the lump in my throat because I could do with one of those right now. The only difference was that Nick always needed a drink or, at the very least, constantly seemed to have one.

My hand still in his, he threaded his way toward the bar, it was like the parting of The Red Sea. He was so used to it that he probably didn't even notice or maybe he did and was glad there weren't dozens of groupies trying to hang off him.

I shouldn't have looked ahead. I should have looked anywhere else, but I couldn't get my eyes off the fabulous rear end that left the Instagram pics of Bieber's butt for dead. I stopped myself from swooning.

Nick signaled to the bartender, a rockabilly gal I'd seen

around town. She nodded, then picked up a bottle of Cointreau in one hand, Jose Cuervo in the other, and poured. Clearly a pro, she worked quickly, made eye contact, and smiled in a way that made her job look easy.

I tilted my head toward Nick's. "You didn't ask what I wanted."

"Margaritas have always been your favorite."

"True."

He edged nearer, so close it made my skin sizzle. I hadn't seen him for four months while the band had been touring, then only briefly yesterday and now this. He shouldn't have any effect on me. This shouldn't be happening.

"Where's Scarlett tonight?" he asked.

"Babysitting. Mom couldn't help out because it was her book club night."

"Is she coming later maybe? Scarlett, that is."

"Nope."

I gritted my teeth because I should have known better. Nick still didn't get it even after all this time. Leaving Thomas with my sister, Scarlett, was one thing. Leaving him with some random babysitter was another, and I wouldn't trust my son to just anyone even if I could afford it.

My breath quickened, my shoulders stiffening. One way or another, Nick always got me worked up. If it wasn't Thomas, it was something else. Damn it, I should never have come tonight.

Thank goodness for the cocktail. The first sip tasted good. The second hit the spot. I pressed my eyes shut for a moment so I could enjoy the alcohol settling in my stomach. After a deep breath, I pulled myself together again.

Meanwhile, the bartender passed Nick his beer, then placed her hand over his, a sly smile on her lips. "No need to pay. It's on the house."

He knocked back a shooter, reached for his beer, then laughed. She exchanged a knowing glance with me, and I laughed too because it made for a nice change to see someone ribbing Nick instead of crawling up to him because he sang in a rock band.

She served the next customer, and I looked away. Not at Nick. I couldn't spend all my time staring at him like some lovelorn schoolgirl.

I'd worn a pair of killer heels to try to make myself feel better—and also taller—because I needed all the help I could get in that field. They were indeed a killer, so I slid onto the ripped vinyl of one of the padded red stools by the bar. These things must have been here since the bar opened a few decades ago.

The Swamp was a dive, and also part of Frankston, part of the fabric of our city, our history too. Even the walls told a story, one wall in particular that was covered in band posters. I'd always liked the black-and-white-checkered floor tiles, but they'd had their day, and I'd never understood the sheets of old newspaper stuck between the ceiling beams. What was that all about? The other walls were black, peeling in places to reveal the white plaster beneath.

Nick pushed the long, brown hair from his face. "Isn't this place just how you remember it?"

Deep and somehow soothing, his voice made me melt. And we weren't even talking about anything vaguely personal.

"It is." I forced myself to think about the subject at hand. "Only more so."

"That's exactly why The Swamp needs me. The previous owner was getting too old and wanted out. He'd let the place run down."

I raised my eyebrows. "No kidding?"

Serious now. "I didn't want The Swamp to go to some developer who'd bowl it over or someone who'd turn it into a Disney version of The Cavern Club." He held a hand out. "Not that I'm saying we're like The Beatles. We're not. But this is Frankston, and this town is rock 'n' roll."

I couldn't deny it. "True."

"I've got plans."

"What kind of plans?"

"I haven't finalized everything yet."

That meant he hadn't started. Nick was always full of big ideas. Not full of shit though. He'd been incredibly focused, put everything into the band, and they'd been a huge success.

I looked around. "Is this really what you want?"

"Yeah, it is, Lily."

"Then I hope you knock 'em dead."

He grinned. "That's the plan."

"Your dad must be pleased for you."

That wiped the smile from his face. He knocked back half his beer in a single gulp. "You'd think so, wouldn't you?"

"Y-yeah, I would."

I should've known that would be a sore point. I also would've thought his father would appreciate the fact his son was putting down roots back in town. Or something close to it anyway. Despite everything, I didn't want Nick to feel bad about his father. The man simply wasn't worth it.

I tried to think of something positive. "You've got a lot to keep you occupied then. A new bar. An album to record."

"That's the main reason we're here. Well, one of the reasons. We're not going to rush this new recording, so we'll take our time and see how long it takes."

"Quality over quantity."

"Exactly." He gulped back the rest of his beer. "And the touring takes its toll. It's what I've always wanted—don't get me wrong—but it's hard work too. We land in Boston or Rome and then we rush off to the next place, and none of those places is home. It's a weird way to live."

I sipped my margarita. "I guess it must be."

"It's hard on other people too, on Thomas for one."

"Yeah, he's still so little."

"I want you to know how much I appreciate you being there for him. You're a constant in his life. And you're a wonderful mother, Lily, truly you are. Thomas is lucky to have you, and so am I."

But Nick didn't have me, not like when we'd been together. My heart lurched, desperation clawing at my throat. Because we'd had three wonderful years followed by three years apart, and it killed me to think about the number of women he'd probably been with since we broke up.

Thomas was the only reason Nick still saw me. I was the mother of his son, and it wasn't enough. Not nearly enough.

A long sigh left my body. I had my own problems, and

right now Nick was one of them.

I saw a familiar face, relief washing over me right away, because Amber's timing was perfect, so I quickly introduced them.

"How do you two know each other?" Nick asked.

Amber sipped her drink from a straw. "From Dancing in the Dark and also from–"

I coughed loudly so she didn't finish her sentence.

"Sorry, I missed that. Dancing...?" Nick asked.

I cringed because I knew exactly what his reaction would be. He thought my hobbies were flakey and maybe they were, but it was too late to back out.

"It's just what you think it is." I amazed myself with my composure. "There's a DJ, music, they turn the lights out, and we dance."

He raised his eyebrows. "You dance?"

"Yes." I stood my ground. "That's right."

"And it's too scary to have a couple of lights on?" He pulled a face. "Maybe a disco ball?"

Amber put her hands on her hips. "It's so that we can dance the way we want to. With no inhibitions. Then we don't need to feel self-conscious."

Self-conscious was not a term that meant anything to him. Not surprisingly, Nick wouldn't let it go. "In the dark?"

"You might be comfortable on stage in front of thousands of people," I said. "But I'm not. I want to dance and have some fun without an audience. Anything wrong with that?"

"Nope, not at all." His face said something different as he shifted his gaze from me to Amber. "So how do you know each other if this is all done in the dark?"

Amber laughed. "Don't be silly! The lights are on when we get there."

"So you can look at all these people who you don't want to see you."

She whacked him on the arm. "Don't knock it till you've tried it. It's *fun*."

His face lit up. "Is that an invitation?"

Nick at Dancing in the Dark? That was my space, my thing, and my time, and I absolutely could not let that happen.

"No rock stars allowed," I said.

"Then there's no problem because I'm not a rock star. I've got the long hair, though."

He tossed back his hair the way he did on stage, only this time he was making fun of himself.

Amber pointed. "You've got the tattoos too."

Someone tapped her on the shoulder, and she squealed as she threw her arms around a couple of long-lost friends. Hopefully that conversation was over.

I held my hand out. "Not one word, Nick."

"I wouldn't dream of it." He drew me in with those blue eyes. "Look, I'm teasing but I'm serious too. We're back for at least six months, and I want to make the most of it. I want to spend more time with Thomas, so I can be a proper father to him."

My heart swelled and sank at the same time because I wanted the best for my son, no matter how hard things were for me with Nick.

"You're a good father, Nick. Problem is, you haven't been around much. Your job isn't exactly nine to five."

"Well, all that is changing."

For now. But it wouldn't last.

Nothing lasted when it came to Nick.

CHAPTER TWO

Nick

So good to be back, even better than I thought. Frankston had a reputation for being nineties Seattle in the middle of nowhere—because we had more than our share of artists, actors, musicians, you name it—but mostly people didn't get it because they couldn't see that our location helped make this city so great.

We were isolated, stuck in northern Nevada, and we'd always had to make our own fun and get creative. In his place, you could dream. Like I'd always dreamed of owning a bar, this bar, in particular.

And now I was back home, I could finally spend more time with Thomas.

I looked into Lily's soft brown eyes. "Thomas is a great kid."

"He is." She couldn't stop smiling when I said his name. "A four-year-old boy is also a handful."

Her eyes didn't look so gentle anymore and maybe she had a point, but if I didn't know what it was like for her, she didn't know what it was like for me either.

"I know this is hard for you."

She nodded. "It's a good thing my family helps out so much, or I'm not sure what I'd do."

"And I appreciate it." I was lucky the Novaks were there too. "Look, I know my family doesn't do jack shit to help, and I'm sorry. I'm not *them*. I want to do a better job than my father did. I want to be there for Thomas."

Something tugged at my heart every time I thought about the little fella, and contrary to what Lily might believe, I thought about him all the time. I'd be tuning my guitar, and I'd see his little face in front of me. Cooper would smash the drums, and I'd remember Thomas' performance with the pots in the kitchen.

My throat tightened. I thought about Lily a lot too, despite the fact I did everything humanly possible to keep her from my mind. You'd think being on the road and having women throw themselves at me would be a pretty good distraction, but it never seemed to work that way.

I nudged her. "I got off to a good start, didn't I?"

Yesterday, the first thing I'd done when I got into town was dump my suitcase, grab the one thing I needed from my place, and head straight to Lily's. Thomas came running down the front path with that wonderful, high-pitched, "Daddy, Daddy, Daddy." The most wonderful words in the universe.

Lily's eyes widened. "He was so happy to see you."

I grinned, couldn't help it. "He loves the new bike. The training wheels make him feel so grown up."

"Yeah, he was blown away."

"He was so good at the burger place too. He said he's never been there before. Is that right? I thought that was a bit weird when he loves burgers and fries so much."

Lily lowered her gaze. "We go … somewhere else."

"Afterwards, he thought going on the swings at night was the most exciting thing ever."

"It might've been a bit *too* exciting."

"What do you mean?"

"He was all jittery and overexcited, couldn't get to sleep."

That could've been due to the evening exercise or it might've been thanks to the chocolate milkshake he'd asked for on top of all the food. I might be guilty as charged.

"I'm sorry, Lily."

She held a hand out. "No, it's okay. I'm just saying."

You'd think I'd have the hang of this fatherhood thing after four years, but I didn't. I hadn't had nearly enough practice.

That was the thing, though. I shouldn't be practicing. That was my kid, my life, the only chance I had. Four years had gone by since his birth, and I didn't even know how that'd happened.

"I'm pleased you're back and you'll be spending more time with Thomas." Lily practically forced the words out. "Really I am."

I'd been hard on her in the past, and that was where that was staying. In the past. Because I was turning over a new leaf.

Austin pushed his way through the crowd toward us. It was hard to miss him with that quiff and the red and black bowling shirt, his idea of casual.

Lily's face lit up as she threw her arms around him, making me wonder why I didn't have that effect on her. He hugged her right back. Old friends.

She held him at arm's length. "So good to see you."

And she meant it.

"You too," he said. "You've grown."

"What can I say? Stilettos are a girl's best friend." She was petite yet somehow, she took over the room. "I could still whip your ass if I wanted to."

"No doubt about that! I bet Thomas has grown since the last time I saw him. Nick's always talking about him, showing off the photos on his phone."

Austin wasn't just one hell of a bass player but a mind reader too. Such a relief to have him sticking up for me.

I shrugged. "I can't help it if he's a good-looking kid. Takes after his mother."

She gave a shy smile. "He's got your blue eyes, Nick."

"And your hair."

Lily had the most beautiful, wavy, light-brown hair. Funny but I'd never noticed until I saw the same curls on Thomas and somehow, Lily grew to become more gorgeous in my eyes. Thomas got a lot from her, his temperament, for one thing. Just as well he wasn't a hothead like me.

Austin looked around. "I can't believe you bought The Swamp. Man, this brings back memories."

I laughed. "Sure does."

He leaned close to Lily, chatted with her for a bit, then said something that made the two of them laugh. A pang of jealousy cut through me. He seemed to have something with Lily that I didn't and maybe I wanted more. Maybe I wanted all of her. Because there was only one Lily even if I didn't want to admit it.

"Do they still have bands here?" he asked me.

"Sure do." I motioned the other way. "Band room is still there. Come and take a look."

He glanced in that direction, then turned to the bar, his eyes widening in a way that might be good or bad, I wasn't sure. Maybe he'd seen someone he knew.

"Ah, sure, I'll join you in a sec," he said.

I placed a hand on his back. "You look like you need a drink."

"Yep." He gave Lily a quick kiss on the cheek. "Catch you later."

Her smile reached her eyes, a wonderful thing to see, even if I wasn't the one who'd put it there.

I took her arm. "I'll show you the band room."

We edged our way through the crowd. It was less crowded as we stepped through the doorway and as I saw the stage on the other side, the memories came flooding back. Of playing here and doing other gigs. A lot of gigs. We'd play at any shithole that'd have us. We'd been shafted plenty of times too when other people would keep the cash that was supposed to be coming our way.

It was different now. The Merchants of Menace had made plenty of money and everybody wanted to be our friend, but it hadn't always been like that. Anyone who said life at the top was hard was lying. It wasn't easy. Nothing was easy, but it beat the hell out of all the shit that had come before.

Barely seeing my son for four years, that'd been hard. The toughest. Getting zero recognition from my father had been tough. And making our way up in the business had been brutal too, no denying it.

"Niiick, my man!"

Lachie came up, gave me a fist bump, followed by one of his cool handshakes.

"And Lily." He held his arms open for her to hug him

which she did, of course, because no woman could resist his surfer looks.

"I've arranged for a little something."

As he said that, my rockabilly bartender Tara appeared with a tray of shooters that she placed on a high table beside us. There was another table and some stools on the other side of the doorway and some assorted crap on the stage. Not much else here.

"Clever." I grinned at Lachie. "Shooters, and I'm paying for them."

"I'll make you pay one way or another, my man. Bet I can drink more of these than you can."

He knew I couldn't bear to lose. "You're on."

I grabbed a shooter and knocked it back. Lachie did the same. The first one went down easily. The second was quicker and the third was a treat.

Lily didn't say anything. She didn't need to.

He motioned toward the stage. "Reliving old times, eh?"

"Yeah, they weren't all good times."

And the shooters made everything so much easier to handle.

I sidled closer to Lily, trying to make her feel more at home. "You never saw that crappy old band of ours, the first band."

"I was underage," she said.

"So were we!" Lachie laughed. "Man, we were beyond bad. We were the pits."

The two of us had started writing songs together back in high school, then found another couple of guys for our first band. No one had ever told us you couldn't have a huge rock band from Frankston, which was just as well.

We didn't have a band like the one we wanted, so we created it. But hey, maybe we didn't get it right the first time. So what?

I shrugged. "Everyone's gotta start somewhere."

"No wonder the crowd threw all that stuff at us."

I'd never forget that night. I'd said something that got the audience riled. Couldn't even remember what. Not that that there was much of a crowd, but those fuckers had gotten angry and started throwing all kinds of crap at us.

I pointed my finger at Lachie. "You told 'em that if they were going to throw shit, they should throw it at me, not you!"

He shrugged, a smile tugging at his lips. "Seemed fair."

"Fair, my ass."

"You were loving it."

And I had been. That's how twisted I was. Because getting a reaction had been all that mattered.

"Some guy came right up to the stage and tipped his beer over your shirt." Lachie doubled over with laughter and had to wait before he could speak. "You brought your shirt to your mouth and said you were going to suck it off."

I laughed too. Whether they were good times or bad, they were *our* times. Lily smiled wanly and maybe I couldn't blame her for not getting it.

That was the night I knew I wanted to be the front man and sing my guts out, no matter what. Crap had rained all over the stage: cans, bottles, assorted other shit. Then I caught a bottle in one hand. My moment of success, my major league baseball catch, and I hadn't even needed a glove. Maybe the audience had wanted to kill me—I'm not sure—but in my head, I had them in the palm of my hands. Insane, I knew.

Lachie had another shooter. "And now you've given them all what for."

Not everyone. Not the one person who counted, the one person who wasn't here, who was never here.

I knocked back my drink and felt something surging through my body—power, revenge—I wasn't sure what.

"Fuck 'em." I leaned on a stool, accidentally knocking it over. It took a second for that to register, then I kicked it across the floor because I was pissed or pissed off or both. I grabbed a shooter glass and threw it across the empty room to the stage. I laughed. So id Lachie as he joined in.

A stool was next as I flung that across the room, then stomped across to the stage where I picked it up and slammed the piece of shit down so it smashed into pieces.

Suddenly the room wasn't empty anymore. Beside me, Lachie pulled down the parachuting that hung from the ceiling over the stage. A dumb idea anyway. Some of it fell on me so I laughed and ripped another hunk off.

People had gathered around. They were cheering, and I was back at that early gig, a crazy kid on the stage, finding my way, trying to work out what the hell to do.

"More, more." Was that what they were saying? Lachie and I were going for it on stage, sweating and laughing, just like old times.

Then someone shoved me in the shoulder. Hard. It was Tara, the bartender, her eyes on fire.

"Enough!"

One word and Lachie and I stopped in our tracks, that was how scary she looked. Suddenly I felt like a teenager caught smoking pot by the cops in the biggest trouble of his life.

"We were just having a little fun." I didn't even know why I was making excuses. "Hey, this is my bar."

"And I won't have you disrespecting my place of work."

"What the...? I'm renovating the place anyway."

"Yeah, and I have to work here until then. You can't do this, Nick."

I wanted to argue with her, truly I did, but all that came out of my mouth was a croaked, "Okay."

She ushered me down from the stage while Lachie stood there, looking like he was going to crap himself from laughing so much. At least one of us was having a good time.

Tara headed for the door, yelling out to the bystanders, "Come on, guys, there's plenty of drinks at the bar."

People moved away, and I headed in only one direction. Toward Lily who was trying hard not to look pissed off but she'd never been very good at covering her feelings.

"Thanks for the drink." She placed her empty glass on the table. "You were right. Margaritas are my favorite, but I've got to go now."

"What?" I spread my arms and quoted an old cliché. "The night is still young."

"It's a shame Thomas doesn't know that. He gets up early."

Which meant she probably had to get up at the crack of dawn too. Another thing I'd forgotten, another reason for me to despair. Sometimes I wasn't sure if I should know better or if she should relax more. Just for one night. Was that too much to ask?

I spread my arms. "Aw, come on, Lily."

"You're drunk, Nick."

"I'll be sober in the morning. I'll be there for Thomas. I'll take him for a swim."

She raised her eyebrows. I knew 'disapproving' when I saw it.

"A swim?" she said.

"Yeah, he'll have a ball."

Her lips tightened. "You'll be careful, won't you?"

"Of course I'll be careful. You should come along." I didn't add the rest – *if you think I can't take care of him.* "Then you can see for yourself."

"I'm definitely coming along to make sure Thomas is okay, especially if there's water around."

"What?" I spread my arms. "Like you don't trust me with him?"

"That's not what–"

"You can't stop me from seeing my son."

Her eyes were two warnings. "Have I *ever* stopped you from seeing Thomas?"

She jabbed a finger at my chest, and I deserved it. I didn't even know why I'd said such a dumb thing, but that stuff just came out of my mouth when I felt she didn't have faith in me.

"You're acting like a dick. Goodnight, Nick."

Lily stormed to the door, weaving through the crowd, pushing past anyone who got in her way. My heart twisted because I couldn't let her go, not like that.

The bouncers practically sucked in their guts to let us pass. She stopped outside the door when she saw I was following.

"It's late," I said. "I'll walk you to your car."

I knew her too well. She wouldn't want to make a

scene in front of the security guys, not when they'd hear every word she was saying.

She took a deep breath, forcing a smile to her face. "Thanks, that'd be nice."

The cool night air sobered me up as we started walking and I told her, "I'll make it up to you tomorrow, and Thomas will have a great time."

"Yep, he'll like that."

"And you?"

"Yeah, I'll like it too. As long as you're sober."

My skin prickled, but I had the self-control not to respond when it would only make things worse. "So how are Scarlett and your mom doing?"

"Good. Mom is amazing with Thomas. You know how happy she is to look after him. Nothing is too much trouble for her."

I saw her car parked on the street not far ahead. "That's wonderful."

Tonight hadn't gone the way I'd planned. I'd had this grand vision of showing how far I'd come and how I was back here to do the right thing, for a while anyway, for as long as I could stay.

Then it hit me. Cooper hadn't made it tonight. He was our drummer, part of the band, and we were keeping him close for as long as we could.

Lachie was here though, helping me screw things up with Lily, or maybe I'd done that to myself. And I was never sure what to make of Austin.

I cleared my throat. "So, ah, what did Austin say to you earlier?"

"Nothing."

"Didn't look like nothing."

"He asked if I ever felt out of place."

I shrugged. "A silly question."

She stopped by her car, staring at me. "I said *all the time*."

My throat tightened. I didn't even know why Austin would ask that or how she could give him that answer when she'd been to The Swamp heaps of times before and she was there with friends. With me.

Something was up with Austin, for sure. With Lily too. I knew she had a lot on her mind with looking after Thomas and me coming back and intruding. At least, that was probably how she saw it. But she could cut me some slack.

I didn't even know what was going on with all these women busting my ass. First Tara, now Lily.

Always Lily.

CHAPTER THREE

Lily

This was a mistake. I should've known better, but Thomas had been so excited about going swimming with Daddy that it'd seemed impossible to back out. My own fault. I should've asked which pool Nick had in mind.

And now here we were.

I was reclining on a banana lounge by the pool at Nick's parents' place, though thankfully they were out. My shoulders scrunched, muscles tight, I forced myself to relax which was all wrong. I wasn't laid-back at the best of times, except perhaps when I was doing stuff with Thomas. That was when I was at my best.

Thank goodness I had the big sunglasses to hide behind. Nick didn't. He didn't even look hungover, which rankled even more. How could he look so damn good all the time?

"Look, Mommy!"

Nick stood by Thomas' side while he crouched beside a garden bed, holding a worm high in the air between his little fingers. I didn't even know where his soft, pale skin came from, when I was olive-skinned and Nick seemed to be permanently sporting a light tan.

"Wow, pumpkin, that's a big one," I said.

"Sure is." Thomas looked so proud. "What should we do with it? Daddy, do you want to eat it?"

Nick nudged his hand away. "Worms aren't for eating, silly."

"They eat them in some countries."

"Not in Nevada. We should put this little fella back in the ground. Earthworms are very good for the soil. They tunnel away in the ground and add all sorts of nutrients."

Thomas' little eyebrows went up in the middle. "What are nuchients?"

"It's stuff that makes the soil healthy. Like when you eat fruit and other good foods that help to make you strong."

Thomas nodded earnestly. Didn't matter that he probably had no idea what they were talking about. Nick was so good with him, and Thomas was so cute, it warmed my heart to see them together. Made me wish things could always be this way.

Sometimes I thought I should've gone to college straight from high school and other times, like now, there was no way in the world I'd swap this for anything. Anyway, I couldn't blame Thomas for that. After high school had finished, I'd been having too much fun hanging out with Nick and working as a receptionist. He was a year older than me, and it had all seemed so glamorous. My own fault, my own decision.

Then, after having a baby, everything changed. I'd been grateful to be able to keep my job with a wonderful boss who was happy to have me work part-time.

Only problem was, now I wanted to go to college

more than ever, wanted to make something of myself, but I was on my own with a child to look after.

Thomas stood and pointed to another section of the garden. "I think we should dig here."

He picked up his red plastic shovel and rushed across all of three feet to the next designated section of his dig.

I got up, smoothed down the loose, white shirt I was wearing over my bathing suit, and wandered across to join them. Nick's eyes were on me, my heart racing a hundred miles an hour as I came closer.

I wished he wouldn't look at me that way. And I wished he would. I wished for a lot of things I couldn't have.

It wasn't as though Nick was my first boyfriend—I'd gone out with another guy for a year when I was sixteen— but somehow everything that'd happened before paled into nothingness in comparison.

Everything since too, if I was going to be honest. I'd dated a couple of guys over the past few years, and at the same time, I'd known they wouldn't last. I'd barely call them relationships compared to the way I felt about Nick. Or used to feel. Because I couldn't let myself get too involved.

He was wearing a pair of board shorts that hugged those magnificent hips. The shorts were new whereas the faded Nirvana tee shirt was not. He'd been so excited when he bought it from a thrift place years ago, back when we were still dating. Vintage, he'd said. That was Nick, effortlessly cool.

I glanced down at the hole in the garden. "Your parents will freak."

He shrugged. "That's their problem."

The gardens were landscaped to perfection, the lawn immaculate, and even the tennis court had been swept of leaves.

"They'll make it your problem too," I said.

"I gave up caring what they think a long time ago." He spread his arms. "Besides, they hardly ever use the pool. It's always too hot or the water's too cold or something else gets in the way. You know what they're like."

Unfortunately, I did. They liked me well enough, or as well as they liked anyone else, but they acted as if I'd given them a grandson when they were way too young to have one. Somehow it always ended up being all about them. As if there was some huge hardship, and Thomas was just some pesky child.

I couldn't understand them, not one bit. It wasn't fair that Nick's dad didn't make the most of his grandson when my dad had died way too young, and he would've loved Thomas to bits. Instead, my dad had never gotten to hold him as a baby or play with him. It was too sad for words.

No wonder I didn't exactly feel comfortable at Nick's folks' place, but that was a much safer option than any of the public pools in Frankston. The thought of those places crowded with people and not enough lifeguards sent a nervous shiver up my spine.

At least here there was no noise, no distractions, and I could keep an eye on Thomas as soon as he went near the water. Much better for him to dig up Grandma and Grandpa's garden. At least one good thing was coming out of that. It made me smile.

Thomas was concentrating hard on his digging when he accidentally flicked some soil into Nick's face. Quite a feat because Nick was six feet two.

"Dude, you gotta be more careful." Nick wiped his eyes.

Thomas looked up. "Sorry, Daddy."

Nick shook the dirt off the red shovel and handed it back to our son. "How about you put this back with your things and we go for a swim?"

"Yeah!"

Thomas raced across, doing exactly as he was told, and waited by the side of the pool in his trunks and Spiderman rash guard to protect him from sunburn. He was a good kid. I'd taught him never to go near water without an adult.

Nick ripped off his shirt, revealing his strong, tattooed arms and smooth, tanned chest. It sent a sizzle up my spine, a sensual one, a reaction I shouldn't be having.

He took Thomas' hand. "Let's use the steps, eh?"

Thomas was waist deep on the second or third step, the world's biggest smile on his face, when Nick let go of his hand to dive in. For those few seconds, Nick's head was underwater, and he didn't have his eyes on Thomas. He couldn't.

My heart jumped to my throat. I'd warned Nick about that before, about how quickly a child could drown, how it could happen in an inch of water. I took a deep breath, trying to calm down, and stopped myself from overreacting.

Seconds later, Nick was standing in the water, facing Thomas. "Now it's your turn."

"Okay." But he just stood there.

Nick shook the hair from his face, water and long, brown hair flying everywhere.

"You're splashing me!" Thomas complained.

"Come on, dude. Jump in. Then you'll be wet too."

Thomas pinched his nose with one hand, reached out with the other, and leaped ahead, sinking underwater. My heart sank with him. Nick was right there, I told myself.

And he was. He grabbed Thomas under his arms and pulled him closer. He was grinning through the water dripping down his face, his hair wet, pale curls sagging.

"I did a big dive," he spluttered. "Just like you, Daddy."

The two of them started playing a game where Nick tossed him in the air and caught him. Thomas loved it, the air filled with his giggles, the most wonderful sound in the world.

Now that they were in the water together and he was with his dad, Thomas had no fear. No, *I* was the one filled with fear. The world's biggest scaredy-cat when it came to kids and water. A wimp.

All because of a bad experience with water when I'd been a kid. Several bad experiences, actually. And they'd stuck with me.

"Mommy, you should come in too," Thomas called out in his high-pitched voice.

Yeah, I should, so I slid the white shirt off my shoulders and edged closer to the steps. Nick's eyes were on me, heat pooling deep inside me. Maybe I should have worn a less revealing bikini, but I hardly ever went swimming and only had one swimsuit. Besides, I liked it when he looked at me that way.

We paddled around, the three of us, and Thomas was so excited, it was contagious. My heart swelled, and we became lost in the bliss of the moment. The feeling was so pure and honest, almost primal. Before I'd had a child, I hadn't known that particular sort of joy existed. I sure as hell did now.

"Watch me swim to the steps, Mommy."

He did his own version of swimming which involved Nick giving him a little push and propping him up out of the water before he reached the end. Thomas pulled himself onto the step and turned, grinning with pride.

Nick edged closer to me. "You look a little anxious. Is anything up?"

My nerve endings skittered, and I didn't know if that was due to Nick or the water or something else. "No, I just think Thomas needs to get out of the sun and back into the shade."

"Sure."

It was only May and not nearly as hot as it got in summer, but the sun still had a bite to it. Nick wrapped Thomas in a towel and started drying him, then looked up at me, smirking, so I knew something was up.

"You know this'd be much safer if we did this in the dark."

I frowned. "Sorry?"

"You know, like dancing, one of those things you do in the dark."

Now I got it. I opened my mouth to argue, then saw movement from the other side of the pool as Nick's parents arrived. My heart plummeted like I was falling off a cliff. I didn't have the stomach for them right now.

Thomas ran up to greet his grandmother. It took all the poor kid's self-control to wait until she'd put down the tray of gin and tonics in her hands, and then he had to wrap his arms around her legs because she didn't believe in bending over.

"Grandma, you're here!"

"Call me Janice, sweetie," she said. "I've told you before."

She didn't like to be reminded of her grandmother status. I didn't mind if he got that wrong.

Nick's parents weren't even that old, only in their fifties, but his mother insisted on Botox and fillers which seemed ridiculous when she was still a good-looking woman.

She gave Nick a hug and waved hello to me, a big smile on her face. His dad followed close behind, dragging a mysterious box behind him. Another expensive gift, no doubt.

Taking a deep breath, I told myself this was their house, and they had every right to be here. Even if that wasn't how I wanted to spend my afternoon.

CHAPTER FOUR

Nick

Dad came across and shook my hand as if I were a business acquaintance. It rankled, there was no denying it. And no changing it.

He was smiling, which made for a pleasant change, as he called Thomas over and pulled the cover off a large item he'd left on the patio. His eyes wide, Thomas knew something was up.

"Ta da!" Dad lifted the cover to reveal a red and blue ride-on electric car.

Thomas jumped up and down and hugged my folks who actually got down to his height to let him do so, a feat in itself.

I thanked them. Lily thanked them. Thomas thanked them a hundred times.

I tried to stop the frustration surging inside me, but this was my childhood happening all over again. Mom and Dad were happy to give the kid over-the-top gifts, but they couldn't see there was no point if they weren't willing to give him the one thing that counted, their attention.

Dad spent all of thirty seconds showing Thomas how

the car worked, propped him up in the driver's seat, and turned his back on him to sit on a banana lounge next to Mom.

Sometimes I wondered if they'd like me to call them Paul and Janice too.

I knocked back a gin and tonic because, hey, that was why they'd brought them out, then joined Lily who was sitting on a wicker chair by the table. She'd thrown that white shirt over herself which was a shame because she looked fabulous in a bikini.

And I knew exactly how good she'd look out of it, how amazing she used to feel in my arms, how good we used to be together. I knew it all too well.

"Not on the grass, darling," my mother called out, and that was about as grandmotherly as she got.

Thomas sat in his car, beaming. "Grandpa Paul, come closer and watch me race."

"I'm having a rest." Dad waved him off. "You play with the car."

I couldn't hold back where my father was concerned. "I thought that since you were here, you'd want to spend some time with Thomas."

"Of course we're here. It's our house."

More of that frustration simmered inside me. "You said you'd be out all afternoon."

"We came back."

I'd called my parents before I landed in town, then again yesterday, but their schedules had been very full at the time, certainly too full to see me or make time for Thomas. Some other important social event must've been cancelled and here they were.

Dad was right, though. They were allowed to come

back if they wanted to. It was just that if I'd known, I would have let Lily know they'd be here and maybe I'd have psyched myself up for it too.

Thomas came running up. The kid ran everywhere.

"Mommy, can I have a drink please?"

"Would you like a snack too?" she asked.

"Ooh, yes, please."

I knew where he got his lovely manners from. Lily. He sat at the table with us, trying to look very grown up, while Lily produced a drink bottle and container of crackers and chopped up fruit for him. These were exactly the sorts of miracles that happened when she was around.

Mom sat up on the banana lounge and lifted her sunglasses, squinting as she looked at the other end of the garden. "You haven't let that child dig up our beautiful garden, have you?"

That child…

Lily stiffened beside me. I placed a hand on her arm to let her know I'd handle this even though I was as riled as she was.

Sometimes I didn't know how I did it. Or how they did it. Every time I came back to town, I made the same mistake because each time I thought Thomas might be a way of bringing all of us closer together.

"You've got it the wrong way around," I said. "It's your grandchild who's beautiful."

My mother rolled her eyes. "Oh, darling, sometimes I think you misunderstand on purpose."

"Do I?"

"Of course we love Thomas. We just don't like him digging up the garden. If we wanted the garden dug up, we'd get a dog."

"Luckily, there's no need now," Lily said under her breath, making me smile.

Beside me, Thomas had a strawberry in one hand, a piece of apple in the other.

"We are *so* busted," I said to him.

He looked around innocently. "Busted? Is something broken?"

I ruffled his damp hair. "Nothing to worry about. Grandma doesn't appreciate our digging in the garden."

Leaning across the table, he yelled out, "We put the earthworms back. So there'll be lots of nuchients."

"Pardon?" Dad sounded confused. He'd never get it. "Why don't you go play on your new car, Thomas?"

"He's eating," I said.

My father leaned forward on the banana lounge. "Speaking of new cars, when will you be getting one?"

Another of Dad's bugbears because, apparently, someone with as much money as me shouldn't be driving around in an old Jeep, the same Jeep I'd bought before I left town in the first place. He'd bought me a BMW in high school, a car that'd been totaled, hit by a drunk driver while it was parked by the side of the road. And Dad couldn't understand that I didn't want a new car when I was hardly ever here anyway.

"I'm still saving up." I knew that would annoy him.

Lily smothered a giggle.

"Your sister just bought a new Mercedes." Dad had probably been dying to tell me that.

"You'd think it'd be easier for her to take the subway," I said.

Another giggle from Lily.

Still, I was serious. Sophia was a stockbroker living in

Manhattan. What was she going to do with a car other than pay ridiculous parking fees?

"I think you're doing that on purpose, Nicholas." Dad put on his stern voice. "Sophia is doing very well for herself."

And I wasn't? I held back the anger flickering in my stomach, the years of angst, years of never living up to my father's expectations.

Sophia was the dream daughter, everything my parents had ever wanted, and I was … I was something else. Sure, I'd been a bit of a nightmare growing up—always acting up, getting into fights, starting fights half the time—but anyone could see that was classic attention-seeking behavior, not that I'd realized it at the time.

Besides I hadn't been a kid for a long time. I had one of my own, in case they hadn't noticed.

I drummed my fingers on the table and looked across at Lily. She mouthed something to me, and I could tell she wanted to get out of there.

"Thomas, how about I put your new car in the Jeep and then you can play with it at home? You can drive all over the grass, anywhere you want."

"Ooh, yeah, Daddy." He swung his legs under the table. "Is that okay, Mommy?"

"Absolutely," she said.

Lily enlisted Thomas' help in packing up their gear, and I stepped closer to my parents.

I looked down at my father. "You didn't make it last night?"

"To that dump?" He scowled. "No, I didn't make it."

"I wanted you to see the bar before and after the renovation, so you can see what I've made of the place."

"Why would I want to do that?"

I gritted my teeth. "You were always telling me I should get into business. Well, now I have."

I'd always wanted to open a bar and have something that was mine and also part of Frankston. And The Swamp wasn't just any bar. I'd never had much of a family, damn it, so at the very least I'd like a sense of community. Something to come home to.

Other than Thomas, of course, my main reason for coming home. And Lily.

I was flooded with the strangest feeling of certainty. That wasn't just about Thomas. It was about Lily too because I couldn't think of home without thinking of her.

"Where's your business plan, then?" Dad asked.

I'd renovate the place. I had a plan. Of sorts. I just didn't have a good answer for him right now.

Dad screwed up his nose. "Didn't think so."

"We're off now." Lily slung her backpack over her shoulder, took Thomas' hand, and led him away. She couldn't get away fast enough, and I didn't blame her.

"I'll be right there," I said and turned to my father. "What are you scowling at?"

"A bar isn't the sort of success you should be chasing. Look at your sister and the career she's built for herself. Look at the way I worked my way up in real estate. Owning a bar isn't a proper job."

"In case you haven't noticed, I've got a job that pays very well. The band."

I'd made more money with The Merchants of Menace than Dad had in the last two decades, not that he hadn't made a truckload himself. I used to think money was the one thing he could understand. I wasn't so sure anymore.

He sipped his drink. "A bar? Great, you've found another place where you can drink. It's a bad move. An alcoholic buying a bar, that's got disaster written all over it."

Fury rolled in my stomach. At that moment, I wanted to shove his gin and tonic down his throat. Wanted to let him know how it felt. Suddenly the idea of doing something I'd regret didn't seem like such a bad idea.

I clenched my fists. I turned. I picked up the damn ride-on car and I left. One way or another, I'd give that man what for.

By the time I reached the edge of the house where Lily and Thomas were waiting, my chest was heaving from anger, not exertion.

Lily looked up at me. "You okay?"

"I should be asking you the same thing," I said.

Thomas stood in a sprint starting position on the side path. "Can I run, Mommy?"

She nodded. "Yep, just stop at the end and wait for us."

He was off, and right away I smiled and started to relax. It was amazing how calming just watching him could be. I lowered the ride-on car to the ground.

Lily looked tired, and I couldn't blame her. My parents were enough to suck the life out of anybody.

"I hope you don't mind if I just want to chill at home with Thomas for the rest of the afternoon, just the two of us," she said.

"No problem. Do I wind him up too much?"

"Yes… No… Sometimes. He needs some downtime, that's all. Look, I know you think I'm a flake because I'm not cool like you and I go to Dancing in the Dark and I have a crazy Croatian family and—"

"No way. Seeing my parents only makes me appreciate your family all the more. If I ever said your family was a bit crazy, well…"

"You did."

"Then I meant it in the nicest way possible."

"I'm not offended. I'm just saying."

Thomas turned to face us from the other end of the path, caught sight of his car, and raced back.

"Maybe you should ride the car back," I said, but he was in the driver's seat before I'd finished the sentence.

I motioned for Lily to walk with me. "For the record, I don't think you're a flake. Well, hardly at all. Look, maybe we can do something together tomorrow evening, just the two of us."

"Sorry, I'm busy."

"Any chance I could tag along?"

"No."

I did my best hip-hop move. "I might be able to dance in the dark."

Deadpan. "It's a slam night."

"What's that?"

"A poetry and stories slam night."

From the look on her face, she was only telling me that to shut me up. It did, but not for long.

I cleared my throat. "Wow, I didn't know there was such a thing."

"Like I said, I'm busy."

"Maybe we can catch up during the day then."

"I'm working tomorrow."

"Okay, how about if I take care of Thomas for the day?"

"You'd have to pick him up at eight. I can't be late for work."

"Eight o'clock, no problem. You got it."

Though she didn't look convinced, she didn't argue either. She took Thomas' little hand into hers. He stepped out of his car and waited at the top of a small set of steps. Sometimes when I looked at him, I couldn't believe he was mine. Ours.

I shifted my gaze to Lily as she spoke to him, but I didn't catch the words. I'd been kidding myself that the band was everything, that this new record was important, that I was finally realizing my dream of owning a bar.

Because everything I'd ever wanted was standing right in front of me. Thomas. And Lily.

That previous sense of certainty warmed me, made me buoyant, gave me hope. I knew. I felt it deep in my heart.

It had always been Lily. I just hadn't seen it before.

CHAPTER FIVE

Lily

I couldn't believe I'd fallen for his nice guy routine. Again. I'd already called. I sent another text message. For all the good it was going to do.

Scarlett looked up at me from the other side of the breakfast table. "No answer?"

"Nope."

"Would you like me to call Mom for you?"

"Thanks for the offer, but I'll take care of it."

She raised her eyebrows. "How about if I blast Nick when I see him next?'

"Absolutely!"

It was so good living with my sister for more reasons than one. She got it. I didn't need to explain everything to her.

People said we looked alike and we did, only Scarlett had the better end of the bargain with the supermodel figure while I got the stretch marks. But I wasn't going to waste my energy feeling sorry for myself. I was going to put all my energy into being mad at Nick.

Thomas sat cross-legged in the living room playing

with his blocks. I gave his little shoulder a squeeze as I headed for the bedroom with my phone.

I called my mom who was on standby to look after Thomas today because I'd had a horrible feeling this thing with Nick would fall through. She was cool about the last-minute babysitting because she couldn't get enough of Thomas. Most of the time, she was more excited than a little kid when it came to, well, looking after a little kid. She was retired, she told me. What could be more important than looking after her own flesh and blood?

She hadn't been so cool when I'd told her I was pregnant. Had gone ballistic, in fact. I could understand she'd been upset about her eighteen-year-old daughter getting knocked up, but I'd been in shock about the whole thing too. She hadn't let up about it. What was I going to do now? So young, only a child myself. How would I ever make it to college with a kid to look after? Hadn't she told me all about contraception? I couldn't explain it. Still couldn't.

Then there'd been a complete turnaround when she'd laid eyes on Thomas. Much earlier actually. And I was lucky to have such a fantastic family.

I tried Nick one more time, my heart rate rising with every ring of the phone. It went through to voicemail. I took a deep breath and steeled myself because otherwise I'd sound like some sort of fishwife, or worse, a crazy Croatian.

"Nick, it's me. It's eight fifteen, and I'm going to be late for work. I'm taking Thomas to my mom's place, then heading to the office. If you get this message, please call me."

Nick had done a lot for us. Buying this house for me

and Thomas to live in, for one thing. He'd been so thoughtful too, looked for somewhere near my family because he knew that was important to me, then he'd made sure both Thomas and I liked the place. Thomas had only been a baby at the time, but still.

And when Scarlett broke up with her boyfriend last year, Nick had been cool about it when I asked if it was okay for her to move in. He wouldn't even let her pay rent or anything.

He could be incredibly generous.

And also an asshole.

Anger burned inside me, and I was mad at myself for showing so much self-control. When did Nick ever show any restraint? Screw him.

I called him and left another message.

"On second thoughts, don't call me. EVER."

I stomped into the living room where Thomas was waiting patiently for Daddy to collect him. My heart broke into a hundred pieces before I'd even said a word to the poor kid. That was the hard part, the part Nick didn't get because he only had to deal with the fun bits of parenting.

I crouched beside him, eyeing up the bag I'd already packed so he'd have everything he needed for the day.

"Pumpkin, there's been a change in plans for today," I said.

The look in his big, blue eyes was wary as if he knew what was coming. "Yes, Mommy?"

"Daddy can't make it today, so I'll be taking you to Granny's instead."

His eyes widened. "But Daddy said he was coming. He told me."

"I know, pumpkin, and I'm sure he'll come another

time, but it turns out today isn't so good."

I saw the breakdown coming and that only made it worse. Thomas' lower lip trembled as he tried to keep it together, but it was like the first tremors before an earthquake. In an instant, he lost it, tears streaming down his pale, chubby cheeks as he started howling.

I hugged his shaking body. "I'm sorry, honey. Daddy can't help it. He's sick."

"Daddy's sick?" Thomas' voice cracked with concern. "Is he in hospital? Is he okay?"

"He's not in hospital, silly billy. It's not that bad. He's not feeling very well and has to rest today. We'll wait and see. He might be better in the afternoon. You never know."

I was hardly lying at all because I had no doubt Nick was lying in bed hungover as all hell. He'd probably gone out drinking with the boys last night and had forgotten about everything else. And everyone.

That was when I decided that if he didn't pick up the phone later that morning, I'd go around to his apartment during my lunch break. If he wasn't awake, he would be by the time I'd finished with him. Awake and very sorry.

CHAPTER SIX

Nick

I'd messed up. Again. I'd already made it up to Thomas by spending the afternoon with him, which had been part of my plan in the first place until things had fallen apart.

Thomas had been fine by the time I picked him up from his grandma's place at eleven even though his grandmother hadn't been fine and neither had Lily. No, when I'd returned her call, she was what I'd describe as absolutely fucking furious.

And she had every right to be. She'd calmed down by the time I dropped Thomas off at home and besides, whatever she was feeling, she never let it show in front of Thomas. I had to admire her for that.

She'd also made it clear dinner was out of the question. Not a problem because it was well after dinnertime now.

I paid the cover charge and wandered inside the bar, grateful no one had recognized me so far. I'd gone to a lot of effort tonight, wearing a vintage suit jacket with thin lapels and a pale-blue shirt, the sort of thing Lily would say brought out the blue in my eyes, or at least that was what she might've said once.

And I wanted her to say it again, wanted to make a good impression, especially after I'd screwed things up today. No wonder I was on edge tonight.

It was dark inside The Silver Swallow, but a huge painting on one wall was lit up like something from an art gallery. A moody piece in shades of black and white and gray, the painting stood out against the burgundy wall. Very cool. Seriously impressive, in fact.

The nightclub district had changed a lot in the last four years, so I figured the place must've been new, but you wouldn't have thought it to look at the interior. It was my kind of grungy.

With a very mixed crowd. I was amazed at all the people who'd come out on a weeknight to a slam night, of all things. An older guy got off a barstool, his arm outstretched for a handshake. So much for not being recognized.

"I just wanted to say I'm a big fan."

I shook his hand. "Thank you."

"I love the way you sing and yell at the same time. You sure can holler, son."

Which was true. I could howl out the words, and I could also croon with the best of them. It all depended on the song.

Laughing, I turned away. "I'll take that as a compliment."

I spotted Lily at a table in the far corner, sitting with the friend I'd met the other night. My stomach did a little flip at the sight of her, which might not be very manly but hey, manliness was overrated. I swallowed, my mouth suddenly dry because the only thing I was certain of right now was that Lily was not going to be thrilled to see me.

Putting on a big smile, I strode across. "Lily."

She looked up. Did a double take.

I leaned over and gave her a one-armed hug before she could stop me, also so that I didn't have to see the pissed-off look on her face.

"And Amber, hello."

Her eyes lit up. "You remembered my name."

"Of course I did. How could I forget?"

I leaned across and kissed her on the cheek, bringing a big smile to her face. Any friend of Lily's was a friend of mine, and I needed an ally.

Lily forced a smile. "Nick, what are you doing here?"

Leaning closer, I whispered, "You can't still be mad?"

"No, not at all."

"I'm sorry. What happened today won't happen again, I promise."

The look on her face told me she'd heard it all before, and she had. I'd gone out with the boys last night and had gotten so drunk I was practically comatose, my way of coping with my father. Not a good way, but my way.

Sometimes it felt as if everyone was mad at me. My father was permanently pissed because I was a continual disappointment to him. And now Lily was angry and disappointed and probably a lot of other things too.

I could be such a prick sometimes, and it made no difference that I didn't mean to be.

Time to take control. "What would you like, ladies? Margaritas?"

Lily opened her mouth to argue but Amber spoke first. "Ooh, yes, please."

"I'll be right back."

I didn't have to wait long at the bar, and I had to admit

this was a very civilized set-up. Muddy Waters was playing in the background, people were chatting, and there were no sweaty drunks picking fights. Made for a pleasant change.

Picking up the two cocktails, I nodded toward my drink to indicate I'd come back for it shortly. I left a lavish tip, not that it was hard to be generous when you had as much money as I did. And I appreciated it. I may never have been stone-cold broke, but there'd been plenty of lean times before The Merchants had hit it big.

I placed the margaritas on the table in front of Lily and Amber. "Here you go."

I felt a tap on my shoulder. I turned to see the smiling bartender passing my drink to me, which wasn't why I'd left the tip, but it was appreciated nonetheless.

"Your mineral water, sir."

"Thanks." I took a seat next to Lily, taking off my jacket because it was kind of warm in here.

She raised her eyebrows. "Mineral water?"

"Yeah, I love mineral water."

"Sure there's nothing else in it?"

I pointed to the glass. "Only bubbles, a lot of bubbles. That's what makes it so refreshing."

Amber sipped her drink. "That's not very rock 'n' roll."

"That's me," I said. "Mr. Meek and Mild."

She laughed. "No way, you're so funny! Ooh, I got an email today with a sneak preview of the line-up for The Flats. I was so relieved to see The Merchants are headlining, but I want to know what took you guys so long."

The Salt Flats Festival was our version of

Lollapalooza, only not quite as big. Who needed Chicago, Paris, or Berlin when you had Frankston, miles from anywhere in Nevada? The Flats was part of the city, one of the things that makes Frankston what it was.

"We played years ago before we had a name," I said. "Then we always seemed to be touring somewhere else."

Also Brett, our manager, had said it was better to wait. He'd been right about everything else, so we'd gone with it.

Amber shrugged. "I was probably too young to go back then."

"I'm sure The Merchants will make up for it." Lily turned to me. "So how did you find this place?"

"I worked it out."

"You Googled it?"

"Yeah. Frankston isn't that big. I could've asked around if I'd had to." More loudly, I asked, "What's the drill tonight? How do things usually work around here?"

Deadpan, Lily said, "I thought you'd know, Nick, you know since you're so interested in poetry. I mean, why else would you have come?"

Amber leaned forward. "It can be such fun, depending on who's on that night. Anyone can get up, doesn't matter if you're a truck driver or a comedian. And you tell your story, something honest or funny or bold. Other people read poetry."

I narrowed my eyes. "And are you bold?"

She smiled. "I might get up tonight. Lily said she–"

Lily whacked her arm. "I'm here to support Amber. If you want to get up, honey, I'm right behind you. I'll listen and clap. I'm with you all the way."

I wasn't letting Lily get away with that. "Were you

going to get up there too?"

She put her hand on her chest. "Me? No, I'm just watching. And supporting."

Amber nodded, rather too vehemently. "Yep, she's here purely in a supporting role."

Lily turned to me. "Whereas you, Nick, I didn't know you were into poetry."

"Yeah, sure I am."

"Do you have a favorite poet?"

"Well, um, not exactly." I had to think quickly. "But I write lyrics. It's not that different."

"Then you should get up." She turned to Amber. "Don't you think?"

There was much nodding and agreement, which was not what I had in mind at all.

"I don't think so," I said. "I don't have anything prepared."

"But you've got so many songs with lovely lyrics," Amber said.

"Maybe another time. This should be *your* night to get up there, and we'll be your cheer squad."

"I like the idea of a cheer squad. In fact…" Amber looked around, then got up. "Might be time for me to get ready."

"Knock 'em dead," I said.

Lily squeezed her friend's hand. "Good luck."

I sipped my mineral water, telling myself it was better than beer. It didn't work, but I was determined not to let Lily down again.

As I put the glass down, my hand brushed against hers, and she didn't pull away. A small thing. A big thing too, and I wasn't going to take it for granted. It was a start, even if she wasn't exactly falling into my arms.

"I never knew you were into poetry and stories," I said.

She shrugged. "If I can, I try to go out on a weeknight sometimes. It suits me. Scarlett's looking after Thomas tonight, and I don't want to ask her to stay home on the weekends. She needs to get out too."

I pointed to the stage. "Do you ever get up there?"

She shook her head.

"But you write a bit of poetry?"

"Poems are short. Something I can do in my spare time. I'm never going to write a novel, and I wouldn't have time anyway."

"You've got a more important job," I said. "You're a mother. And you do a wonderful job with Thomas."

She beamed, deservedly so.

"I mean it." I slid my arm around the back of her chair, feeling a lot like a teenager making a move on a first date. We'd had a first date once. We must have.

That wasn't the bit I remembered, though.

I remembered breaking up. Things falling apart. Lily saying she never meant to get pregnant. Me telling her I'd had a big part in that too. After that, I'd been away so much with the band touring, taking all the gigs we could get, trying to make our name, make some money. That was where all my energy had gone, not into Lily and Thomas, not then anyway.

This was now. My big chance. I was right beside her, and she hadn't moved away.

"You can write poetry and be a mom," I said. "You can do anything you want."

"Easy for you to say."

Not necessarily. There was a lot that hadn't been easy for me either, but I wasn't going to go there now because that wasn't what this was about. She'd stopped so I gave her the space to speak.

"It's good getting back into some writing, just ordinary stuff, even the sort of writing we used to do in high school."

I nodded. "Yeah, sure."

"It has helped me get into the swing of things."

"What things?"

She sucked in a deep breath. "I'm thinking about college. I'll need to know how to write, you know, essays and things."

A breakthrough. The pieces started to fit into place.

I drew her into my arms and gave her a hug. "That's wonderful."

She broke off the embrace, dropping her hand onto my thigh, almost as if by accident. I was closer to her than I'd been in a long time, and it filled me with warmth. Warmth and something else.

She pulled her hand away to sip her margarita, then left her hand on the table. I covered it with mine so she knew I was here for her.

"So you're serious about renovating The Swamp?" she asked.

She might've been changing the subject, but she wouldn't be getting away from me.

"I'm still working it out. Buying the bar seemed like a good idea at the time. Having a bunch of ideas in my head is one thing, but that's only the start. I guess I thought this was something I'd be good at because I'm used to drinking at a lot of bars. Doesn't work that way. Running and renovating a bar is a different thing altogether."

She laughed, and I wasn't even making a joke.

"I'm glad you're honest about it."

I nodded. "Now I've got to make it all happen."

"Would your father help, you know, if only to point you in the right direction? He must have connections or know someone who could help?"

Clearly, she hadn't overheard the conversation I'd had with my father yesterday. It still stung so I wasn't going to get into that now.

I shook my head. "Some things you've got to do on your own."

Lily pointed to the stage. "Hey, Amber's up there, along with some other guy."

The emcee introduced a dumpy-looking bald dude who looked like he was wearing his grandmother's cardigan. He had guts, I had to hand it to him. Though I didn't catch all of his poem, I clapped at the end because he deserved it for getting up on stage. I knew exactly how hard it was to put yourself out there.

Amber was next, one hand draped on the microphone as she tried to relax. She told a story about being on vacation and taking a river cruise where she drank too much and ended up in the men's room, then pretended to stand at the urinal for a couple of minutes before racing out of there. She got a big laugh from the audience and a giant clap from our corner.

You could see the relief on Amber's face as she stepped off the stage. Also a sense of achievement.

She was beaming as she walked over to our table. Lily got up to give her a hug, so I took the opportunity to wrap my arms around both of them. Any excuse.

Lily held her at arm's length. "You were great, Amber."

"Funny too," I added.

"Thanks." Amber turned to me. "This is kind of surreal for me, on stage one minute, getting a hug from Nick Steel the next."

"It's okay," I said. "You can call me Nick."

Her eyes were wide. "You're almost like a normal person."

"Hey, I'm just a guy."

"You don't act like a rock star, not when I'm talking to you." Amber's expression turned serious. "Then again, you did trash the bar the other night."

It was exactly the sort of dumb thing I did when I'd been drinking too much, and now it seemed kind of lame.

I swallowed. "Yeah, there was that."

"Like you were Johnny Depp or something. I didn't think people did that stuff anymore."

I held a hand out. "No need to rub it in."

Two friends waved to her from the bar, and Amber said she was going to catch up with them. I didn't mind. It was just me and Lily again as we sat back down.

"Are you really serious about college?" I asked.

"Yep. I've thought about it. If I get a job as a teacher at the end of it, I can still have vacations with Thomas. That'd mean a lot to me."

"Frankston College?"

"Where else? I can't leave town. I haven't quite worked it out yet. There's Thomas, my job… That's the hard bit."

"Quit. It's only a job."

"It's not that easy." She glared. "I need the money."

"I can help. If this is what you truly want, we can work something out."

Silence. I'd said something wrong.

"I still care about you, Lily. You're the mother of my child. I'm supposed to take care of the two of you."

That didn't begin to cover it—I wanted her in every way that mattered—but I didn't want to race too far ahead and scare her off.

Meanwhile, more silence from Lily. Surely, she couldn't object to my helping her out with college.

She reached for her purse. "I should get going."

I got up, grabbed my jacket, and took her arm in a way she couldn't possibly refuse. "I'll walk you to your car."

We said goodbye to Amber and stepped out into the cold night air, freezing for that time of year. I draped my jacket across Lily's shoulders, walking slowly by her side to try to make our time together last longer.

Her car was parked nearby. Unfortunately. And we reached it in what seemed like about two seconds. She pressed the unlocking mechanism.

"I'm trying to understand, Lily, truly I am."

She looked up at me with those gentle, brown eyes. "You don't have to worry. I can never be mad at you for long, Nick."

"You've got a lot on your plate. Do you have regrets? Is that it? About having Thomas so young?"

"Thomas is the one thing I will never regret, not in a million years."

"I feel the same way."

And me? Did she regret me?

Cupping her chin in one hand, I leaned over and placed a kiss on those soft lips, the lips that had once belonged to me. She didn't flinch, didn't push me away. A relief. Sometimes I wasn't sure what to expect from her.

Then I kissed her the way I wanted to, the way I used to, the way she deserved. I held her close as if I didn't want to let her go, and that was the truth. I didn't want to let her go. This felt so right, not because she was the mother of my child but because she was Lily.

Eventually we broke off the kiss, and she was all misty-eyed, her face flushed, lips still parted. I'd had that effect on her, and I wanted to do a hell of a lot more to her.

"Lachie and I are working on some songs at my place tomorrow," I said. "Not that we're going to be awarded a Pulitzer, not like Kendrick."

Her mouth fell open. "Kendrick Lamar? You're on a first-name basis?"

"I've met him once or twice." Now I sounded like a douche, and that wasn't what I'd intended. "I'm free after three. Come over any time after that."

I saw the uncertainty in her eyes. "You'd like me to drop Thomas off?"

"Both of you. We'll go to the park or something."

She got into the car and looked at me through the open door. "Sure, Thomas would like that."

And you, Lily? What would you like? What are your dreams, and do they include me?

The questions I didn't ask.

CHAPTER SEVEN

Lily

Nick had said three o'clock, hadn't he? We were in the music room at his apartment—sound proofed, of course—and it was now well after three. Thomas and I sat on one side of the room, Nick and Lachie in full swing on the other. Lachie strummed chords on guitar while Nick played the keyboard, singing a few notes or words, then writing them down because this was a song writing session.

Thomas had been watching wide-eyed, staring at his daddy like he was some sort of superhero, but that could only last for so long. I could tell he was waning. Surprising he'd sat still for this long, in fact.

Nick didn't notice, though. He was in his own little world. Sometimes the only person he had to think about was Nick. He didn't need to worry about Thomas because I was always there for our son and always had that side of things under control. A shudder of resentment shot up my spine. Jealousy too.

Thomas leaned closer. "I'm thirsty, Mommy."

I motioned for him to get up. "Sure, honey."

In the kitchen, I grabbed a glass and lifted Thomas up so he could hold it under the cold water dispenser on the stainless steel fridge. Maybe I was a tiny bit jealous of the top of the range appliances too.

After he finished, he held his glass out. "More please."

I tickled him. "You just like using the dispenser." He giggled as I lifted up him up, then became serious again as he used the machine, and I lowered him to the floor.

Nick had only been back a few days and already the kitchen was covered in empty beer cans and bottles half full of liquor, and probably wouldn't be tidied up until the cleaning lady came. It'd sure be nice to have one of those.

I took Thomas' hand, and we went back to the music room. Nick held his hand out for Thomas to give him a fist bump, then played something on the keyboard, singing a tune over the top.

"That's not the way you did it earlier," Lachie said.

Disappointed, Nick raised his eyebrows. "I know. I don't have any scrambled eggs."

He looked across at Lachie, then at me, or rather, at the puzzled expression on my face.

"An in-joke," he said. "I usually come up with some working lyrics, until I write the proper lyrics. When McCartney wrote *Yesterday*, at first he called it *Scrambled Eggs* and kept singing it that way until he came up with the lyrics."

Nick's granddad had put him onto The Beatles years ago, and now he was their biggest fan. It didn't matter that the songs were old, not to a music nerd like Nick.

Thomas jumped off his chair, a big smile on his face. "I can sing a song about scrambled eggs."

"Really?"

"Yes, really." He was nodding wildly, then composed himself and started singing. "*Scrambled eggs/ Yummy when they're runny/ Scrambled eggs/ Yummy in your tummy.*"

The song stopped rather abruptly, and Thomas stood there expectantly until we all clapped.

Lachie grinned as he turned to Nick. "I think you could learn a thing or two from this fella."

"That was fabulous, Thomas," Nick said. "Lovely singing."

"I made my song up quickly, Daddy." His little eyebrows went up in the middle. "How come it takes you and Lachie so long? Is it because you're not very good?"

Leaning over his guitar, Lachie cracked up laughing. Me and Nick too. Meanwhile, Thomas looked so innocent as he stood there trying to work out what was going on.

"Did you like my song?" he asked.

"Sure did." Still grinning, Nick turned to Lachie. "I think we should call it a day. Next time we come back to this, we'll be fresh. We can work it out then."

Lachie placed his guitar in the case on the floor. "Yeah, I think those creative juices have dried up."

That was one of the things about Nick that I'd forgotten, the time and energy he put into the band, into writing songs, practicing his craft. The songs didn't come from nowhere, and they didn't start off as a polished, finished version. It was all part of a process, and it took time.

Earlier, I'd been miffed that Nick had been ignoring Thomas, but now it hit me that this was his job, one he took very seriously.

Nick called Thomas over. "Do you want to play some keyboard?"

Thomas ran over and threw himself onto Nick's lap. His answer.

"Same time tomorrow?" Nick asked Lachie.

"Sure thing."

Lachie gave me a quick kiss on the cheek, then saw himself out while I settled back and watched my two boys as they mucked around on the keyboard. At first, they competed to see who could make the biggest, loudest sounds, then they moved onto some nursery rhymes. Thomas fluctuated between gleeful giggling and expressions of supreme concentration as he mastered the keyboard.

This was so pure, so much fun, such a pleasure that I was flooded with contentment. If only things could always be like that.

After a while, Thomas had had enough, got a bit wriggly, and climbed down from Nick's lap.

"Wow, you were really good on the keyboard," I said.

Thomas beamed. "Thanks, Mommy. I've been sitting for a long time."

"Y-yeah."

"And I need to stretch my legs." He put on a bit of a show by lifting his arms over his head and holding the pose. "I think I need to go to the park."

I stifled a giggle.

Nick said, "The park, eh? I think that can be arranged."

"Yay!"

There was some jumping up and down—from Thomas, not Nick—and the three of us headed off. Nick took the new bike with training wheels out of my car. Thomas hadn't let me leave home without it. Luckily, he was still getting used to it so he wasn't racing too far ahead of us as we walked behind him.

Nick lived in a nice part of town, one of the more expensive parts of Frankston in a new, very expensive apartment block, whereas I preferred my location closer to my mom's house.

"You were so lovely with Thomas back there," I said.

Nick shrugged. "I'm not a brilliant keyboard player but even I can do *Mary had a Little Lamb*."

"A bit of guitar, some drums. You're very musical."

"I only took up the drums because I knew it would drive my parents crazy." He snorted. "It worked."

"I'd forgotten."

"Forgotten what?"

I shot him a superior look. "That you're such a nerd."

"Hey, what are you talking about? I'm not a nerd."

I poked him in the side. "Yes, you are. You used to spend all your time holed up in your room playing guitar and writing songs. At school, you spent more time with Lachie than you did with me."

"There was never anything going on between me and Lachie. Big difference."

I should've been happy for Nick and his success. Instead, sadness tugged at my heart. He'd put everything into the band, and there hadn't been much left for me, or at least that was the way it'd seemed. We'd tried for months, both before and after Thomas was born, and it hadn't been enough. We'd been too young, too stupid, and maybe we were never meant for each other.

I told him, "I remember how many afternoons you spent rehearsing with The Merchants."

"We wanted to be good."

"And you gave it everything you've got."

He stopped to help Thomas cross the road, then took the bike as Thomas got off to run across the grass to the playground.

Nick looked ahead. "We want to go back to those old times, that excitement and rawness. The band is slicker now, but we don't want to forget where we came from. We can be even better if we get back a small part of what we used to have."

A part of what we used to have...

If only he were talking about me. My breath caught in my throat. I shouldn't let myself think it or hope or go there. The disappointment would be too much for me, and then I'd shatter into a thousand pieces. It was hard enough to keep myself together as it was.

"That first recording we did was the best," Nick said. "We want to get that same sound back into the new album."

Yep, the album, the band, these were the things that mattered. I respected him for that, truly I did. It was just everything else that was so hard to handle.

Thomas clutched the chain of a swing, waving wildly at Nick to come and push him. Nick rushed over while I wandered to join them.

A woman not much older than me stopped pushing her daughter so the swing slowed. Her eyes were wide and firmly fixed on Nick. "Oh my God, you're Nick Steel."

"Don't tell anybody." He tried to laugh it off.

"Can I get a picture with you, please? This is too much. I can't believe... Oh, my friends are never going to believe this."

She reached for the phone in her pocket, fumbled,

then bent over to pick it up.

Nick held a hand out. "Sorry, not now. Maybe another time."

Which surprised me. He was usually so obliging.

Her mouth fell open, so he added, "I'm with my little boy. This is my family time. I hope you don't mind too much."

The woman nodded, didn't seem to quite understand, then her little girl started tugging at her hand and saying something about ice cream.

Nick waved as they left. "Have fun." He gave Thomas a little push on the swing. "How high do you want to go?"

Thomas grinned. "As high as the sky."

Another push. "Higher than the clouds?"

"Yes, push harder, Daddy."

"What about as high as outer space?"

Thomas swung into the air. "Yes, as high as a rocket ship."

Maybe I should've been worried about Thomas being pushed too high, but I wasn't. Water was the big worry for me. Always had been. I shuddered at the memory of having my head held underwater.

Then I threw that feeling off, refusing to think about it, and gazed at Nick and Thomas. My heart started to swell right away at the sight of them at the playground, so ordinary and so beautiful. The worst thing was that when I looked at them, I was all too ready to forgive Nick for messing up yesterday. A major screw-up at that.

I kept hoping that would be a thing of the past, that Nick was turning over a new leaf, and I also knew that that wouldn't happen. Nick was Nick. And that could only last so long.

Maybe I should make the most of it. Except I couldn't. Not when it came to Nick and me.

I'd kissed him last night, a big mistake, one I couldn't make again. I didn't know what I'd been thinking. Which was the whole problem. I wasn't thinking. And that sort of thing would only get me heartbroken. Again.

Maybe I was the one who needed to turn over a new leaf and stop making the same mistakes. I couldn't go there, not again. I had to draw the line.

A soccer ball came sailing over from miles away. Nick leapt into the air, catching it with both hands and ending up on the grass. He was such a big kid sometimes.

Thomas slowed on the swing. "Good catch, Daddy."

He was. Way good.

Nick searched for the kids who'd kicked the ball and passed it back to them.

Thomas jumped off the swing and grabbed my hand. "Mommy, why did that lady want to take Daddy's photo?"

"A lot of people know Daddy," I said. "Because he's a musician. The band is very popular, and they have a lot of fans, so people get excited when they see Daddy."

"So do I."

Thomas nodded with the certainty of a four-year-old, serious for all of about two seconds until Nick called him over to the slide, giving his son one hundred percent of his attention. That was the Nick I liked to see, the man behind the myth, the songwriter, father, friend, lover…

My heart clenched. I knew exactly what was happening, and I couldn't help it, no matter how hard I tried to push these feelings away.

Because I was discovering Nick all over again.

CHAPTER EIGHT

Nick

I was so goddamn fortunate in a lot of ways. Our first album had been a hit, and it was just as well because if you didn't make it big right away, the record companies wouldn't give you the time of day. They'd dump you and leave you with bills you didn't know you had. The limo that picked you up, the party they threw for the band, all those things you hadn't actually asked for—one way or another, you ended up paying for it all.

Just as well for us that Brett had gotten in early and negotiated good deals at a time when we hadn't thought we had any negotiating power. That was the power of a strong manager, and we were all reaping the benefits.

Sitting at the dinner table with Lily and Thomas, I had that extremely-fucking-fortunate feeling hard and strong, only it had nothing to do with the band and everything to do with these two.

That hadn't been the way I'd felt when Lily had told me she was pregnant, though. I hadn't known it could be like this.

I'd loved Thomas as soon as I'd laid eyes on him. The

day of his birth was the best day of my life, bigger and better than the record deals and the adoring crowds and the huge gigs, even if I hadn't realized it at the time.

My main problem had been that I'd never wanted to be a father at twenty. I'd wanted to be in a rock band and play gigs and promote our record. So that was what I'd done.

Lily was a year younger than me but had always been more mature, which was just as well for Thomas because I was pretty useless. I was catching up now, though.

I slid a few more French fries onto Thomas' plate. "See, isn't it good when Daddy cooks?"

"You didn't cook, silly." His high-pitched voice cut through the air.

"Sure, I did."

"No, you didn't. You used your telephone. You showed me how you did it."

I was grinning. "Yeah, I cooked using the phone."

He shook his head, light-brown curls flying. "That's not how you do it. You cook in the kitchen. Like Mommy does."

Lily smiled. "Thanks for sticking up for me."

"Mommy, why don't we have Uber Eats all the time?" Thomas' eyes widened. "Then we can have burgers and fries every night."

Thomas couldn't believe it when a delivery guy had turned up with our order. I suspected they couldn't afford take-out, and I was certain Lily wouldn't accept anything vaguely resembling charity so that time I kept my mouth shut.

My mind was still open though. To many things.

Thomas nodded earnestly. "I think Auntie Scarlett

would like this. Maybe we can get Uber Eats with her sometime."

"Maybe." Lily pushed across a plate of julienne vegetables—to me, not Thomas. "Don't forget your carrot sticks."

I reached across and ate one obediently, setting a good example.

Thomas added, "Lots of nuchients."

"Yep." I leaned back in my chair. "Full of nuchients."

Lily's smile filled me with warmth. I loved that I could make her smile. Or was she smiling at Thomas?

Scarlett had gone out for dinner and a movie, so we had plenty of time until she got back. Time for what? That was the question.

After we finished dinner, Lily enlisted Thomas' help in cleaning up. I wiped the table in an effort to appear useful even though Lily had everything under control. Anyone looking in would've thought we were a happy family. I only wished that were true.

It riled me to think about my own dad. When I'd been a kid, he was always working late and on weekends, making a lot of money, building his career, and spending zero time with his family. An absent father.

A bit like me. It got my goat even more that I might be following his example. Unlike him, I wasn't driven by money, but I was certainly driven, and I'd put everything into the band and my music. There hadn't been much left over after that.

Time for things to change.

"Okay, Thomas." I tossed the sponge into the sink. "What's next?"

He came flying over to me. "Dessert."

"Nooo, something else."

"Bath." He lowered his voice, his gaze too. The kid was not impressed.

Earlier we'd been having an intense Duplo session building roads and towers, and Thomas had somehow managed to convince Lily that a bath could wait. She'd explained to me that he loved his bath but was in permanent procrastination mode, so every night she had trouble getting him in there and then could never get him out afterwards.

"How about if I give you your bath tonight?" I asked.

He looked up at me with those big, blue eyes. "But Daddy, you don't know how to do the bath."

"Sure, I do."

No, I didn't. I'd have to wing it. My son was four years old, and I'd never given him a bath. It was a goddamn disgrace. When he'd been a newborn, Lily had tried to get me to do it, but I'd been too scared. He'd been so little, not even able to hold his head up. He hadn't been a baby for a long time though, and I didn't have any excuses now.

Lily ran the bath and came back to the living room while Thomas put away his Duplo blocks, making a hell of a racket in the process.

"Daddy, are you coming to Baba's birthday party?" he asked. "She's going to be nearly a hundred. She's very old."

Lily's Croatian grandmother was indeed very old, but I didn't think she was a hundred.

"I'm not sure," I said.

"You're invited," Lily said quietly. "Mom and Baba both asked if you wanted to come."

I couldn't keep the smile from my face. "In that case,

I'd love to. You sure that's okay by you?"

"One more or less won't make much difference, and Thomas will love having you there."

Not quite the answer I wanted. "So your Baba's not still mad at me?"

Lily stifled a giggle. "I wouldn't say that."

What was that supposed to mean? Surely, if I was invited, Baba must have forgiven me for leaving Lily all those years ago. I hadn't even left her. That wasn't how it'd happened. We'd drifted apart, the band had been touring, and things hadn't worked out, but that wasn't how her grandmother saw it.

I sidled closer to Lily, my arm brushing hers as we watched our son. "He's a great kid. You've done a wonderful job with him."

"It's nice to have you back." She straightened, correcting herself. "I mean, you're good with him too. It's just that you're not around much."

"I'm here now."

I took her hand in mine, our fingers intertwining, while we stood there pretending nothing was going on. It sent a thrill up my spine. Close, so close. Some guys loved the chase and the sense of anticipation. Not me. I knew exactly what I wanted, and she was standing right next to me.

I could have had her once. How could I have thrown it all away? I must've been deluded and driven, and that was no excuse. I'd been a dick.

Thomas wiped his brow as if exhausted after an excruciating day's work, then took my hand to lead me to the bathroom. I loved my son but there was still a sense of loss as Lily let go of my grasp all too easily.

In the bathroom, I helped him take off his clothes and tickled him, only for him to push my hand away. "No tickling till I'm sitting down in the bath."

Who was I to argue?

After he was safely seated, he told me, "You have to sit there."

"Sure." I did as I was told, dropping down onto a blue stool.

"Mommy has lots of rules about the bath and safety and stuff."

"And now we've got to get you clean and washed."

Lily walked past the bathroom door, stopped and looked in, then moved on. She'd always been a bit odd around water, but I didn't mind doing things her way. I soaped Thomas' arms first, then rubbed soap onto his back, pretending to find all sorts of dirty bits, which Thomas thought was a hoot. The soap flew out of my hand accidentally on purpose, and he giggled like crazy. Then came the most hilarious thing of all, a bubble fart, and the kid howled with laughter.

I was laughing too, at Thomas' reaction more than anything, and okay, maybe it was funny seeing the bubbles.

Lily appeared, leaning in the bathroom doorway with her arms crossed. "What's all this noise? This is the noisiest bath I've ever heard."

"It's not a noisy bath. It's a Daddy bath!" Thomas proclaimed, whatever that was supposed to mean.

He splashed around, then stopped, his eyes wide. "I just had a great idea. Daddy should have a sleepover."

My heart skipped a beat. I could've kissed him right then and there. My kid was the best, and right now, he had no clue how good he was.

I shifted my gaze to Lily still standing in the doorway, her face frozen in an uncomfortable smile. Getting up, I stood close to her, close enough to let her know my intentions.

"You can't stay here tonight," she said in a low voice, breathless already.

My heart sank but not for long. "It'd be the most natural thing in the world for me to stay."

"It'd be a mistake."

"You're not worried what Scarlett might think, are you?"

"No, I'm thinking of Thomas. He'll get confused. He's only a little kid."

She was thinking ... too much and that meant she was thinking about it. Her gaze was lowered, her lips parted. So tempting. Not now though, not in front of Thomas, not like that.

Thomas piped up. Loudly. "Why are you whispering?"

Lily nudged me aside, the moment lost. "Sorry but Daddy won't be able to stay tonight, honey."

Thomas pouted, his face clouding over, and I wanted to make him feel better, but I wasn't going to go against what Lily had said because, as parents, we had to be a united front. Even I knew that much.

"Hang on." I put on a bright face for Thomas. "How about if I put you to bed tonight and read you a bedtime story? How would that be?"

He nodded wildly. "That'd be good, Daddy. I'd like that. A lot."

I took my place back on the blue stool. "Okay, then we've got a deal."

Lily tapped me on the shoulder and leaned over. "You

had your back to him. You've got to keep an eye on him all the time in the bath."

I stopped myself from saying we were both here and nothing dangerous was about to happen. I was nothing if not agreeable.

"Sure," I said.

It didn't matter who was right about that because I was sure as shit right about a lot of other things. She was fighting me every inch of the way. I could see that. I could also see the woman underneath who needed to take time for herself, who wanted more out of life, who needed me, damn it.

I was going slowly for now but that wouldn't last. Things were going to change gear soon, very soon.

CHAPTER NINE

Lily

It was only coffee and then he'd be leaving. Nothing to worry about, nothing at all.

I'd stuck my head in the door earlier when Nick was reading Thomas a bedtime story, and my heart had been ready to break. As cute as ever, Thomas was struggling to keep his eyes open while insisting on just a few more pages.

And Nick had loved it every bit as much as Thomas. You couldn't feign that look of contentment. Besides, Nick had never faked anything in his life. That wasn't something I could accuse him of.

There were other things he was guilty of, though. I didn't know how he did it. How could one man look so goddamn sexy sitting on the edge of the bed with a book in his hands?

Now here he was beside me on the couch, as cool and relaxed as always, while I pretended to drink my coffee. I needed to get my mind off Nick and onto the present moment or I wouldn't be able to cope, so I cupped the mug in my hands and took in the aroma. Closing my eyes,

I took a sip and savored the rich flavor, but it wasn't working. My mind was all over the place, so I tried to focus on something positive instead.

I cleared my throat. "It's so good being able to talk to you about Thomas."

We'd been sitting here reliving the events of the day and talking about Thomas in the admiring, devoted, slightly nauseating way that only two parents could. You'd think the kid was a genius to hear us talk about him, and hey, maybe he was.

Despite that, my stomach churned. I'd been so anxious watching Nick give Thomas his bath, and it hadn't helped that I knew that was an irrational fear. For starters, there wasn't nearly as much water in a bath as in a swimming pool, and we'd all gotten through that the other day.

It all went back to swimming lessons at school. They'd been a nightmare for me, all because of one kid, Jared Mills. He'd gotten a kick out of dunking my head under water, and that last time had been the worst. Water up my nose, in my throat, no air in my lungs, not able to breathe, and that horrible feeling of ultimate helplessness. After that, he'd been caught in the act and punished, but the fear had never left me.

It was stupid to be thinking about that now, stupid for me to think about it at all when it was so far in the past, so I gritted my teeth and changed the subject.

"You haven't said much about the bar."

"The Swamp?"

"Well, what other bar would I be talking about?"

He pressed his eyes shut for a moment, and I could see there was a weight on his shoulders. Something was up.

"It's a big job, renovating a bar," he said.

"Yeah, it is."

"And I'm not jumping into it until I have a better idea what I'm doing."

"Sounds fair." I wouldn't have thought that would be bothering him that much. "It's a bigger project than you thought?"

He sipped his coffee then put the mug back on the coffee table. "There's some other stuff going on too. We've got a lot going on. Lachie and I are still putting together the songs for the new album."

"I know. I've seen you in action."

"Sorry if we took longer than we were supposed to." He smiled. "I liked having you and Thomas watching."

I'd liked it too. A lot. And I'd found it hard. It was always like that with Nick. He was the best and the worst of everything.

Thomas... That was who we were talking about. Best to keep the conversation safe.

"You're wonderful with him. I'm glad my family will get to see it too." I paused, not sure if I should go there. "You're like a changed man."

"I hope so. I'm trying, Lily."

"And I appreciate it."

"It's taken a while but I'm more responsible than I used to be. And it's staying that way. From now on, I'm spending more time with Thomas, getting my act together, and being a proper father. We're here while we'll be cutting the next record and that'll take a while which suits me fine. Then we'll have to tour."

His voice was so deep, so mellifluous, and he was telling me exactly what I wanted to hear, that he'd be around and that he'd be with me and Thomas.

I had to focus. "I know you have to promote the record."

"It's not just that. Touring is where the money is. And that pushes up merchandise sales. But after that, we're changing the way we do things. Shorter tours, maybe two or three weeks at a time. And that means I'm going to be around more. We all will be."

Unconvinced, I nodded. Nick had all the best intentions, and I believed he'd be around more and spend more time with Thomas. But I didn't believe it'd be nearly as rosy as the way he described it. Something would come up. It always did.

"You don't believe me, do you?" he said.

I opened my mouth to argue. I hated it when he could see right through me.

Nick reached for my waist, tickled me, and made me shriek. I covered my mouth because I didn't want to wake Thomas up.

I also hated it when he knew exactly how to get to me.

Breathless, I grabbed Nick's wrist. "No, no, you can't do that. I'm not Thomas."

Nick's eyes narrowed. "You're not too old to tickle."

I edged back. "Yes, I am. I am definitely way too old for that."

Everything changed in an instant. He leaned over me while I tried to get away, his hand hovering over my waist, ready to tickle, to make me shriek. He was so close, too close, his face inches from mine, and if I was breathless before, that took it to a different league.

"Scared?" he asked.

I was. Scared he was going to kiss me and scared he

wasn't. Frightened I was going to lose him when he wasn't even mine. Fearful of what was lying dormant inside me, the part of myself that I held back, that I had to keep covered because if I didn't, I'd end up breaking into a thousand pieces.

"No," I said.

He slid his hand onto my waist, made me feel small, made me feel a lot of things I didn't want to feel.

I couldn't go there. Couldn't do that. I stopped breathing.

"Because I'm not going to tickle you." His breath was warm on my neck. "Not unless you want me to."

My mouth went dry. We weren't talking about tickling. We were talking about something else.

He pulled back and edged away from me, taking his hand with him. "If I can't tickle you, I take it a spanking would be out of the question."

A joke. Nothing more.

I forced a laugh, as if I'd been in on the gag all along. I couldn't let him see what was inside, how badly I'd misread the whole situation, how my heart had plummeted.

I didn't know what to say or do so I reached for my coffee mug, picked it up, and put it down again. The last thing I wanted was coffee when everything I'd ever wanted was seated on the sofa beside me.

"You used to be so much fun," he said.

"What do you mean *used to be*?"

"You know exactly what I mean. What happened to that young girl who used to try to keep up with me beer for beer?"

"She grew up, Nick. I can't handle the hangovers

anymore."

I should've been angry. Instead, desperation dripped inside me because he was right. Part of me had been lost, and sometimes there was no going back.

"Come on," he said. "What happened to the girl who flashed her boobs at a cop car that pulled up next to us?"

My mouth fell open. "That was only once."

He nudged me. "And you *didn't* get arrested. That was quite an achievement."

"Don't remind me."

The memories came flooding back. We'd been two young kids hanging out and drinking together and making love. I hadn't cared that I had an uninspiring job and was procrastinating about college. Hadn't cared about the future because I'd had Nick, and he was all that mattered.

He said, "You were always trying new things: belly dancing, bongo drums, drawing classes, macramé."

"I never did macramé."

He grinned. He got me.

I picked up the mug again, desperate for some way of asserting myself. "I'm still trying new things."

"But now you're so shy, like with this dancing in the dark thing."

"You've got it all wrong. It's fun. You should try it."

I regretted the words as soon as they slipped from my mouth because the last thing I wanted was for Nick to show up there.

"There's more to it," I said.

He nodded. "I know. You have Thomas to think about. And Scarlett can help out with babysitting on a weeknight but not so much on the weekend. I was listening, Lily."

As I looked into Nick's eyes, for the first time, I thought he finally got it. There was no complacency or complaining, only a realization that that was how things were.

"I'm sorry, Lily."

"For what?"

"All this time, I blamed you for losing that part of yourself when I was the one who did that to you."

"Not you. Life did that to me."

And having a baby at nineteen. Not that I regretted Thomas, and therefore I'd never be able to regret Nick. Because the two were linked.

And now?

Now I desperately wanted to do something I'd regret.

Nick took the mug from my hand and placed it on the table. He pushed my hair back over my shoulder, sending every nerve ending in my body on edge with anticipation. He wasn't teasing, not anymore.

He cupped my jaw in his hands and looked into my eyes. I saw the young man I'd fallen in love with in high school, the man who'd loved me once and who could perhaps love me again.

He brushed his lips against mine in a kiss that was barely there, and my world changed all over again. His kiss was gentle. As if asking permission. Like he really needed to ask. Couldn't he sense how much I needed that?

He moved away from my mouth and nuzzled into my neck, peppering little kisses along my bare skin. My back arched with pleasure, a sensual thrill shooting up my spine. No other man could make me feel that way. It wasn't just desire. It was so much more.

Leaning forward, he covered my mouth with his and

kissed me the way I wanted him to. We were reclining into the sofa, our tongues rolling against each other, bodies intertwining. His hand was on my waist, inching higher until he was cupping my breast and my whole body was thrumming.

That was what I wanted, his hands all over me, his breath on my neck, his hardness pressed against me. I pulled his shirt up, desperate for more, in need of his skin on my skin. I ripped apart the button on his jeans. Too many clothes.

I didn't know what I was doing.

Tears burned at the back of my eyes, tears of pleasure if there was such a thing, tears of pain because I could never have him, not all of him, not the way I wanted.

I should let Nick go. I should ask him to leave.

There were a lot of things I should do, and I wasn't going to do any of them. Instead, I slid out from under him, took his hand in mine, and led him to the bedroom.

* * *

Nick turned to look at me. I was sitting up, partly covered by the sheet, the night air cool on my bare breasts, while he was perched on the edge of the bed. Naked, just the way I liked him. He'd always been tall, but he'd filled out since I'd last seen him like that, a bit more flesh on his bones, more muscle, more manly.

Leaning closer, he cupped my breast in his hand and took my nipple into his mouth. Heat pooled deep in my belly, but I couldn't go there again. I pushed him away, only for him to tickle my other nipple with his tongue.

"Nick!"

"Hey, I was just kissing them goodnight."

"If you don't leave now, you never will."

"Now there's an idea."

He was already getting up as he said that, reaching for the trunks hidden under a pile of clothing on the floor. He pulled them on, and I stared. I couldn't help it. He looked good in his underwear and good out of it.

And he had to leave. We'd already had the conversation about how he couldn't stay the night—for Thomas' sake. Children needed boundaries and stability so they knew where they stood. I couldn't possibly let my baby get wrapped up in whatever was going on between me and Nick, not when I wasn't even sure myself.

Most of all, I didn't want Thomas to get hurt which was exactly what would happen if he got all excited because Daddy was sleeping over and then all of a sudden he wasn't. Not that Thomas understood about sex because he didn't. But he'd still know something in his world was changing.

Nick was dressed now, grinning. "I'll go home like a good, little boy now."

He leaned over to give me a goodnight kiss, and I savored the moment, the softness of his lips, the firmness of his resolve. Because he had to go. No one knew that better than me.

And that was exactly why that was the saddest kiss of all. He turned away, not seeing the tears in my eyes, the fear on my face as I twisted the sheets in my hands.

He left, and my heart broke into a hundred pieces all over again because I needed him so desperately and I could never have him.

Realization seeped through my skin, sank deep into my bones, my chest filling with a horrible sense of dread. How could I have let that happen? What on earth had I been thinking? I should've been stronger and stood up for myself.

Instead, I'd done the one thing I'd promised myself never to do.

I'd fallen in love with Nick all over again.

CHAPTER TEN

Nick

The Merchants had played some amazing places since leaving behind those early tours we'd dubbed 'Shitholes of America.' The crowds at Glastonbury and Summerfest had been amazing. We'd toured Australia and headlined Splendor in The Grass on the most glorious evening of all. We'd even managed to slip in some smaller gigs that had seemed more personal, where I'd felt I was connecting with the audience, where I could see how much those people loved the band.

So why did I feel that sense of trepidation now? For Baba's birthday party? It was nuts.

Thomas hurtled ahead of us down the side path of Lily's mom's house while I carried some containers of food with Lily ambling along beside me.

I felt like Neil Armstrong. *One small step for a man*, and all that. I saw Sandra, Lily's mom, whenever I was back in town because she looked after Thomas. Hadn't seen her grandmother or the other relatives for years. I hadn't been part of the family for a long time and didn't think I was now either. One thing was for sure, this crowd was going to be a lot harder to win over than the folks at Lollapalooza.

At the end of the path, Thomas crashed into Sandra, which made me wonder if she might've been waiting for him. She was the most devoted grandparent I'd ever seen.

Crouching down, she gave him a hug. "You nearly knocked me over. You're getting way too big."

"Must be my big muscles." He bent his skinny white arm and flexed.

Sandra felt his biceps. "Oh, so strong."

And so cute. It was a wonderful thing to see, truly it was, yet for some reason a wave of anger washed over me. My parents were never so loving and giving with Thomas as that, nowhere near it. Which only made me more grateful for Lily's family because they always seemed to be overflowing with love.

"You know what day it is tomorrow?" Sandra asked.

Thomas nodded wildly. "A special day because you're taking me to the zoo, just the two of us." Turning to Lily, he pointed to the other side of the yard where a couple of kids were hanging out near the slide and sand pit. "Can I go and play?"

She leaned over and kissed him. "Of course you can, pumpkin."

And he was off.

Not far from the little kids, three teenagers were hanging around looking bored or trying to look cool, I wasn't sure which. Other friends and relatives were scattered across the yard, some sitting at the trestle tables that had been set up, others at the rear of the yard behind the shed where I could see a pig turning on a spit. The smoky smell made my mouth start watering right away.

One thing I'd say about Lily's family was that they knew how to put on a spread. There was no expensive catering, no nouvelle cuisine, no caviar or *foie gras*. Nope, at these gatherings America met Croatia, and we ate like kings even though neither country had one of those.

Lily's mom gave her a quick hug and kissed her on both cheeks, kind of a tradition around here. They saw each other nearly every day but never let that stand in their way.

Hands on her hips, Sandra turned to me. "You didn't sleep in today?"

I deserved that. "Nope, I'm never going to sleep in again."

"Ha! I'd like to see that."

"Thanks for inviting me. I really appreciate it."

"What can I say? An eighty-fifth birthday is a big thing and deserves a celebration."

I laughed. "Thomas said she was a hundred."

Sandra leaned closer. "And if you say that to Baba, you'll be a dead man."

"Don't worry, I'll be on my best behavior."

"Lily tells me you've been working hard, writing some songs."

"Yep, it's going pretty well."

I had to hand it to her. Music had never been a big part of her life and her taste fluctuated from middle-of-the-road to soft rock—from Coldplay to REO Speedwagon, maybe with a bit of Michael Jackson thrown in—all of which was as far from The Merchants as you could get. But she always insisted she liked the band and had even come to some of our early, less salubrious gigs.

She raised her eyebrows. "How long does it take to

write a few songs?"

I shrugged. "Well, it all takes time."

"So when are you going to get a proper job?"

"I-I…"

She burst out laughing and whacked me on the shoulder. I couldn't believe how deadpan she'd been just seconds earlier. Sucked me right in.

"I know," she said. "I'm just giving you shit."

I'd always known she could give shit. I'd just never heard her say the word before. She took me by surprise a second time.

I turned to Lily. "Aren't you going to stick up for me?"

"Nope, you're a big boy."

I couldn't make out the look in her eye, maybe admiration, maybe something else. Sometimes I could see right through her, and other times she was so guarded it was hard to tell what was going on with her.

But I was here, and I was going to make the most of it.

Scarlett appeared, a huge smile on her face, as she ushered her grandmother ahead of her. I gave Scarlett a quick hug and kissed her on the cheek because it'd been a long time since I'd seen her, and it was a relief to see a familiar face. In some ways, she was like a taller version of Lily, only blond, and in other ways, the two of them couldn't have been more different.

She held me at arm's length. "Catch you later."

My relief at seeing a familiar face vanished, replaced by momentary panic. "Hey, aren't you going to help me out here?"

"You're on your own." A quick shake of her head and she was off.

Meanwhile, Lily gave her grandmother a big hug,

kissing both cheeks, then holding on to her a bit longer. So funny seeing them together. They were about the same height, only her grandmother was much rounder.

I passed the containers from under my arm to Lily so I could give her grandmother a hug too. My arms were open, but the woman was glaring, so I chickened out and shook her hand instead.

"Happy birthday," I said.

"Another birthday, I'm too old," she shouted, partly because she was a little deaf and partly because Lily's family liked to yell when they were all together.

"Not true. You look better than women ten years younger than yourself. I can see where the Novak women get their good looks from."

She put her arm around Lily. "Not me. This one is so pretty."

In her accent, the word came out more like 'prutty' and I couldn't have agreed more.

"Thomas is such a gorgeous boy too." She drew out the word 'gorgeous' so it sounded like at least five syllables, then resumed the glare. "He takes after his mother, looks just like her."

"But he has Nick's eyes," Lily said.

Baba shook her head. "That's the only thing. Just that one part. Nothing else." She pointed to the containers that were now under Lily's arm. "You didn't bring me presents, did you? I told everyone, no presents."

And she wasn't the kind of woman you argued with.

"Just food," I said.

"Then what are you doing standing here? Go and put that in the kitchen."

Lily leaned over, passed me the containers, and

whispered, "You'd better do as you're told."

"The kitchen." Baba became even louder. "I take you to the kitchen."

Lily and her mom were both smirking when the older woman led me away. I was seriously worried as I placed the containers on the kitchen table because there was no one else around and no escape.

"I want to talk to you," Baba announced.

My mouth suddenly dry, I swallowed. "Great."

"I never see you but Sandra and Lily, they tell me about you, about how you play in that rock band." She spat out the last two words like she was talking about a criminal activity. "And now you come back."

"Yes, I'm back for six months at least, which means I can be there for Thomas, spend more time with him."

She shook her head. "I not talk about Thomas, not now. I talk about you."

I nodded. "O-okay."

"You have a lot of money."

Not sure if that was a question or a statement, I nodded.

"But you have no brains."

My mouth fell open.

She shook her finger at me. "Lily is a wonderful girl and a good mother. Very good. You make mistake. You should have married her a long time ago. I told Sandra that, and I tell you now too. But no, you're too busy, always making noise with that rock band. I know what goes on, drinking and drugs. Don't think that because I'm an old woman that I don't know. I know some other things too."

I nodded because it wasn't going to help to tell her I

found smoking pot boring so I stuck with beer and booze in all its other wonderful forms. Somehow, I didn't think that would go down very well.

"You think you're so smart." She screwed up her face. "What do they say here? This is under your nose and you can't see it. Then no one tells you the truth because you're a big, important rock star. Lily doesn't say it. Sandra doesn't say it, so I have to say it. You're stupid. Now it's said."

My shoulders slumped. The worst thing was I thought she might be right. She'd oversimplified things because life was complicated and neither Lily nor I had planned on having a baby. It wasn't something we'd even talked about. Until we'd had to. And nothing was easy where humans and feelings were involved.

Still, if you cut things down to their simplest level, the woman had nailed it.

"Yes, ma'am," I said.

"I'm not ma'am." She got louder with each word. "You should call me Baba."

Because it was rude for me to address her as anything else even though I wasn't Lily's partner, not anymore. I hated to think what would've happened if I tried to call her Mrs. Novak or, worse still, her first name.

"Yes, Baba," I said.

"Good." Her face softened, and she stretched out her arms. "*Now* you can give me a hug."

Man, was I glad that was over. I bent over and wrapped my arms around her, thinking how strange it was that someone so little and so soft could be so hard.

She stepped away, a sparkle in her eyes. "Thomas might look like you. Just a little bit."

"Thanks."

She pointed to the fridge. "Now get the big bowls of *salata* and carry them outside."

The salad. I was on it and out of the door before she changed her mind or her mood. Outside, people were taking their places at the trestle tables while over on the other side of the yard, a couple of Lily's uncles were cutting up the pig, huge knives in their hands.

I wandered across to shake hands with Lily's grandfather. He'd become even more mellow since being diagnosed with dementia. I suspected Baba had always been the driving force behind that relationship anyway. I asked Lily's uncles if I could help, but these guys seemed to think I was a guest which meant I should sit down and be served.

Baba came over, and in the nicest way possible, yelled at both me and her husband to sit down. He shook her off and moved away at his own pace while she took my hand and dragged me away.

"Vinko never listens," she said.

Brave man, I thought.

"He still wants to work in the garden and do the pruning and the big jobs, but he can't."

"You don't want him working in the yard?"

"It's not just his dementia. He has a bad back. He'll hurt himself, and the tree is too big."

"A tree? You need it pruned?"

She stopped by the table and gave me a look as if to say *hadn't I been listening.*

"I can help," I offered.

Her mouth thinned. "I don't need your money. You can't pay someone to do the job."

Lily had told me how Baba found any sort of paid help around the house to be a personal insult. I didn't get it, but I could roll with it.

"I can come over and help," I said.

Disbelief was in her eyes. "You?"

"Yes, me."

She poked me in the chest, which might've been good or might've been bad. I was getting lost here.

"Daddy, Daddy." Thomas was patting the seat beside him, a big smile on his face because he'd be sitting between me and Lily.

"You sit," Baba said, then left.

Scarlett came up behind me, her hand on my back as she sat on the other side of us, and the first plates of pork started being passed around.

She leaned close, handing me a platter. "You know you have to eat. A lot."

"Yep, I've already been primed."

Apparently, not eating very much or having a small appetite was an enormous insult in the Croatian culture, one I was in no fear of making.

I picked out a piece of pork for Thomas, but he shook his head. "I only want chevaps."

Skinless sausages. I'd had *cevapcici* at Lily's mom's house before.

Lily took the plate from me. "That's okay."

She put some chevaps and salad on Thomas' plate, and we started digging in.

I turned to Scarlett. "Thanks for helping out with babysitting. It's a huge help to Lily, to both of us."

"It's no trouble. Thomas is a great kid."

I nodded like the proudest dad in the world. "I know."

"And I really appreciate the way you and Lily both helped me out when I needed somewhere to stay."

"No problem. It's worked out even better than I thought."

"Remember, you have to eat," Scarlett said. As if I could forget.

Though I felt a bit like a turkey being stuffed before Thanksgiving, I also felt the warm glow of success because I was pretty sure I was approaching the Baba Seal of Approval. I might not have won her over completely, but I wasn't far off, and that told me something. I had this under control. I could do this.

This whole concept of family was something I hadn't understood when Lily and I had first started dating. It wasn't just that I'd been young. I'd been stupid, as had recently been pointed out to me. I got it now, though. If I was going to be part of Lily's life, I had to get along with these people as well.

Thomas was jumping around in no time and bounced away to play at the first possible opportunity. Lily turned her back to me to speak to some relatives on the other side. These were her people, her family, and this was her mother's house, the place she'd grown up. Maybe I was a little bit at home here too.

It filled me with warmth to see her like that. Relaxed. Comfortable. Because she wasn't like that very often, not around me anyway.

And I liked watching her, the smile that reached her eyes, the bounce of her wavy, light-brown hair, the easy way she laughed.

There were loads of other things I liked too, the weight of those breasts in my hands, the gentle dip of her waist, the curve of her butt, the rhythm of her hips, the way she gasped when I entered her and felt as if I might explode then and there.

"You'd better take good care of Lily," Scarlett said.

Surely, I couldn't have been busted. The woman couldn't be a mind reader.

"Don't try to deny it." She gave me a dirty look. "I can work out what's going on."

Lily hadn't said anything or at least I didn't think she would have, but Scarlett would know nevertheless. She'd probably seen my car at the front of their house the other night. And hell, maybe she *was* a mind reader.

"I'm not a twenty-year-old kid anymore," I said. "And I plan on taking care of both Lily and Thomas."

"You'll break her heart, only it'll be worse this time."

That was where she was wrong. There were loads of things that were worse—a life half-lived, not being with the one you love, living your life in fear. To be left wondering what might've been. Wouldn't those things be worse?

Scarlett loved her, I got that. What I didn't get is why these people couldn't trust me a little.

"Has it occurred to you that I might have a heart too?" I asked. "That I might not be all bad?"

"Just don't be a prick, that's all I'm saying."

She sucked the wind right out of me, got me when I wasn't expecting it, right when I thought I had that in the can too. As if I needed more Novak women busting my ass. As if my own parents weren't bad enough. As if I didn't have enough on my plate.

Maybe I'd been going about this all wrong. Maybe I should put all my efforts into Lily and making her feel special. She didn't want to do anything that might upset Thomas—that I could understand—but it was time to make our relationship more public.

All I had to do was convince Lily.

CHAPTER ELEVEN

Lily

Thomas had been going full speed for hours, racing around the yard and playing with his second cousins. I could see trouble coming because later he'd come down to earth with a bang. Sometimes it was as if he had an 'on' switch that went on in the morning and stayed dialed up to ten. This afternoon he was up to eleven, which was worrisome.

He was a skinny, sweaty bundle of nerves twitching on the seat next to me and itching to get up. The problem was, it was so hard to slow him down.

"What if I go and get my special teddy for you?" I asked.

He nodded wildly, water dribbling down his chin as he guzzled from my glass.

I wiped his chin with a napkin. "Would you sit with teddy for a bit and keep him company? Then you can play some more later."

His eyes lit up as he slid off the chair. "I'll go and play now."

I got up too. "Then you'll have a rest when I get

back?"

More enthusiastic nodding. "Yes."

"And soon it'll be time to go home."

"I don't want to go home." He pouted, then I could practically see the light bulb go off in his little head. "I know. I can stay and have a sleepover."

In which case, he'd never get to sleep. "Sorry, pumpkin, that's not happening. I'll get teddy, and I'll be back."

Thomas spotted Nick and went hurtling into his arms. Nick spun him around so there was a lot of giggling and squealing. From Thomas, that was.

Warmth engulfed me, satisfaction settling deep in my stomach, because seeing the two of them together was one of my favorite things in the world. Nothing could touch the deep father-son bond. Nothing would pull them apart.

If only all relationships were made to last.

As soon as Nick put him down, Thomas was off again, and Nick's mind was definitely not on his son as he gave me a lingering look that reminded me of the things he'd done when we'd spent the night together, the electricity of his touch, the way he made me feel.

Sparks started shooting up my spine, then I realized where I was and hoped like hell no one else had noticed what was going on between us. Then again, maybe not everyone could see right through me the way Nick could.

What was I thinking? I wasn't, that was the problem. I had to get my head together. I had to get teddy.

I turned and left, navigating my way past a couple of relatives until I was in the house again, heading for the safety of my old bedroom, except it wasn't my room anymore, something that hit me all over again as I stood in the doorway.

Mom had removed most of the girly things from my teenage years, the pink and purple comforter, the ornaments on the dresser, the band posters and pin-up board filled with photos. She'd replaced the comforter with a blue one so Thomas would feel comfortable when he stayed the night. As it turned out, he hadn't had many sleepovers here and when he had, he'd insisted on sleeping in Mom's bed. Funny kid.

Opening the closet door, I crouched down to reach for my old teddy in a box at the bottom, along with some other items that were still dear to me, my Jesse doll, Barbie and her pink convertible, a delicate, ceramic child's tea set, all things I was saving in case I had a girl one day.

A wave of melancholy washed over me because I'd love to have another child, so much so that sometimes it left me aching on the inside. I shouldn't feel that way when I had a happy, healthy, beautiful boy, and I couldn't have asked for a better kid. But I didn't always have a lot of control over my feelings.

I got to my feet slowly, looking at the photos and flyers and other bits and pieces that I'd stuck on the inside of the closet door years ago.

The centerpiece was an early photo of the band where they all looked so young, even Austin, and he was the oldest. I'd thought they'd all looked so cool at the time, but now it made me smile to see Nick standing in front of the other guys, hands in his pockets, trying to look very rock 'n' roll. He'd only just gotten the tattoo on his right arm and had made sure to wear a short-sleeved shirt that showed it off.

"Hottest guy you ever saw, hey?"

Nick stood in the doorway, his arms crossed, a big grin on his face. I laughed because he was so much cooler now that he wasn't trying to be.

He sauntered across the room to join me, his hands on my waist from behind, his breath warm on the back of my neck.

I stared at the photo. "You look so young."

"We're still young. We've got plenty of time ahead of us."

His voice was so deep and enticing it was hard for me to think of anything except Nick. I pressed my eyes shut as he nuzzled into my neck, peppering tiny kisses along the bare skin with a touch so gentle it was barely there. It only made me want him more, set my nerve endings alight, made me shiver in the best way possible.

His hands wandered higher, edging closer to my breasts, driving me crazy until he was cupping them in both hands from behind, desire coursing through my body. That was the problem with Nick. I always wanted more.

Turning around, I snaked my arms around his neck, held his gaze, and saw the longing in his eyes. I longed for him too, so much that it was killing me on the inside, and it was so hard to stop.

He covered my mouth with his, our lips parting, tongues rolling against each other. Heat pooled between my legs, hot and immediate.

We were in my old room so the memories came crashing back, and I was a teenager again. Making out in the car, on the couch, in the park, everywhere we could until that first wonderful night together when his parents had gone out. The first night of many.

I was a teenager, and I was twenty-three. I was the girl at the front of the mosh pit waving her hands in the air at her boyfriend. I was young and free. I was a mother.

I was the young woman who got left behind while The Merchants toured. I was Cynthia Lennon missing the train when John and the others traveled to meet the Maharishi. The one left behind.

How had all of that happened?

Breathless, I pushed Nick away and looked around. Teddy, that was right. I was getting my old teddy for Thomas.

I must've seemed lost because Nick reached to the floor to pick up the bear. "Looking for something?"

"Someone." I corrected him. "Teddy has a living, breathing, beating heart."

"Hey, who am I to argue?"

I stepped away but Nick sidled up against me, pressing me against the closet door. His chest was hard, his lips soft against mine as he kissed me, his touch electric as he ran his hands all over me.

"We can be quick," he whispered.

I shook my head.

He rubbed up against me. "Or we could take it slow. No one will notice we're gone."

"It's Thomas." I felt like such a frump but said it anyway. "He's waiting."

Nick took a small step back. "I can wait too."

My mouth suddenly dry, I swallowed, trying to get my head together.

He held my gaze. "I'll take you home whenever you're ready. We can have dinner together later, the three of us."

"Scarlett will be there."

"Her too. I don't mind. Then, afterwards…"

"Sorry but dinner won't work tonight. It's Thomas. He gets overwrought and then can't wind down. He seems fine but then he gets jittery, can't sleep, can't do anything." I kept going so Nick couldn't argue. "You're not part of his routine, and it's way too much fun and excitement having you around. He needs some peace and quiet, or he'll be a wreck."

I couldn't believe the words that came flooding out when only seconds ago, I could barely speak.

Thoughtful, Nick nodded. "Okay, there's always tomorrow. I'm meeting Austin at the bar. Maybe we can catch up after that, especially if Thomas is with your mom."

I nodded.

"Let me know when you're ready for a ride home."

Patient. Understanding. Nick was none of these things, yet he was willing to wait. Not for long, though. He had something in mind, for sure.

Meanwhile, I needed time to get my head together. I should never have slept with him, but there was no going back now. What was more, I didn't want to go back. I'd broken all the rules, all the things I'd set in place to protect myself, and now I was lost.

Not that I was weak or couldn't push men away because I could. I'd done it before. There'd been a nice guy called Andrew who'd taken things too fast and practically wanted to be a father to Thomas, and I'd gotten rid of him quick smart, but that was different. No other man made me feel the way Nick did.

As we turned to leave, he grabbed my arm. "I trust you."

And I love you.

My chest was gripped with pain because of the words Nick didn't say, couldn't say, because that wasn't how he felt. He loved the girl I used to be, but those days were over, and I wasn't carefree or young and I couldn't be that person anymore.

He held my gaze. "I'm not leaving you, Lily. Can you trust me too?"

I nodded. Desperation surged inside me because I wanted to trust him. I wanted things to work out between us. I wanted our relationship to be sparkly new.

But you couldn't turn back the clock.

*   *   *

Scarlett had gone out since it was a weekend. She had friends and a life, and obviously she should be out meeting people. She was three years older than me, but she was the one with the youthful life of a twenty-something. Not that I begrudged her. It was just that sometimes I wished it could be me. Was that too much to ask?

Thomas was finally asleep after taking ages to settle. I was in bed too. Pretending to read a book, sitting around feeling slightly pathetic.

I let out a long sigh. It'd been a long day, and it might be an even longer night. I felt a lot like Thomas, a little kid who'd had too much excitement today and couldn't switch off. Restless, my mind buzzing, muscles twitching.

I had a ritual for Friday and Saturday nights. It might not be as exciting as going out to dinner with friends, seeing bands, and drinking too much. But it was what I did to take my mind off that very fact. I chose a movie to watch or picked out a good book and relaxed with a glass of wine.

The book and the wine were happening. The relaxing was not.

I didn't know what'd come over me. Except I did. I was a wreck, and it was all because of Nick, and I wasn't sure how I'd let that happen.

A clinking sound grabbed my attention, making me sit up. Then silence. It must've been my imagination running away with me. I sipped my wine and stared at the book in my lap.

There it went again. I could've sworn I'd heard the clanging of something hitting the window. A chill shot up my spine, an unpleasant one, a warning sign.

I didn't want to investigate. I wanted to curl up in bed, but I was alone in the house with Thomas and I had him to think about. My nerves on edge, I put the glass down, pulled off the sheets, and slid my feet to the floor.

No more clinking sounds. Now it was a definite knocking. Against the glass.

"Lily, Lily."

My name. I breathed a sigh of relief because I recognized the voice. Nick, not an intruder. A burglar would hardly call out my name. Nerves shot up my spine for that very same reason. Because it was Nick, standing outside looking in.

I pulled the window open. "What are you doing here?"

He slid onto the edge of the sill. "Freezing to death while you let me in."

"Why do I have to let you in? Are you a vampire?"

"I might be."

As I stared into those blue eyes twinkling in the dim light, I thought that was the one thing he might be right about.

He didn't wait any longer, swinging his legs around, looking very much like someone who'd had a lot of practice sneaking into girls' bedrooms. Which was strange because even when we'd been teenagers, he'd only ever used the front door.

I put my hands on my hips. "You've never thrown stones at the window before."

"It's never too late to start."

He looked me up and down, his gaze settling on my pink tank top, the shorts hanging off my hips, the exposed skin on my waist, then back up to my face. Despite the fact I was covered up and clothed, I somehow felt as if every layer was being peeled off.

He grinned. "I don't know how you can look so serious when you're wearing pussycat pajamas."

I tried to gather some dignity. "They're called crazy cat shorts."

"Well, they suit you just fine."

I had to laugh because that dignity thing wasn't working for me. "I don't know how I can be the one who's crazy when you came in through the bedroom window."

"Hey, maybe someone should write a song with that title."

I frowned. "That's the bathroom. *She came in Through the Bathroom Window.*"

He touched my nose with his finger. "I know."

Of course he did. He was a much bigger music geek than I could ever be. A bigger Beatles fan too.

As he stepped closer, a shiver shot up my spine, not because of Nick but because of the cold air blowing behind him. My gaze dropped to the drapes dancing in the gentle breeze, and it struck me that if I closed that window it was like an agreement on my part. An invitation.

I closed it.

Nick stepped closer. Tilting my chin up with one hand, he pressed a kiss to my lips. The kiss was gentle. The emotion swirling in my stomach was not. A small part of my resolve melted away.

He beckoned me with his eyes. "This isn't going to be quick."

I pressed my eyes shut. If only I could make this night last, extend our time together, or think of a magic spell so I could keep him in my life forever.

He made me feel the way I did when we were younger. Brought back all those old feelings. And he made me feel like I was a hundred years old, the one who looked after Thomas, the responsible adult.

"We're not teenagers anymore," I whispered.

"We can be. I can be whatever you want me to be."

My chest tightened, the ache in my heart deepening. I was thinking too much, feeling too much. I was never going to get my act together around Nick, not ever.

I pushed him onto the bed. Damn it, Nick was a mistake I'd made before and one I was going to make again.

He was mine. For tonight anyway and I'd make the most of it.

I straddled him, pulled my tank over my head, let him stare at my naked breasts. He reached for them, but no, he couldn't touch. Not until I said. I grabbed his hands, intertwined my fingers with his, and leaned over so my hands were on either side of his head, caging him in.

He was right. This wasn't going to be quick. Tonight, I

was in charge. I'd make him wait, torture him just a little, and I'd enjoy every burning, trembling, sensual moment.

We went at it. On the bed, the floor, me on my knees in front of him, me on top, Nick rolling me over, side by side, we flowed from one thing to another. We took our time. Savored every touch. Let the tension build until we both exploded, then we started all over again.

Eventually, we took a break. A much needed break. I padded to the kitchen for another glass so I could share my wine with Nick. We sipped like civilized people but that didn't last because we weren't civilized. We were hungry, starving, desperate for more.

Nick tipped a little white wine onto my chest. He licked it off. Made his way from my nipples to my stomach, kept going lower, lower, licking and sucking and driving me to the edge until I shattered into a thousand pieces all over again.

I let out a long groan, as lengthy and painful and wonderful as my orgasm. I was slumped on the bed in a pool of sweat while Nick sat up beside me, reaching for the wine on the nightstand. Thirsty work.

There was a knock at the door. I grabbed Nick's arm. Horrified, I froze.

"Are you okay?" Scarlett's asked, concern in her voice. "I thought I heard something."

Great, Scarlett was home, passing my door at that very moment. That was worse than being caught by my mother, and I'd never been caught by Mom. Burning with embarrassment, I had to come up with something. And quick.

"Fine. I was just coughing." I coughed a couple of times for good measure.

There was a pause.

"Goodnight," she said from the other side of the door.

"'Night."

I spluttered and that time the cough was real because I'd been holding my breath and had almost forgotten how to breathe.

Seconds later, I was giggling uncontrollably while Nick pulled me close to stop me losing it completely.

After a while I had my breath back. "I can't believe I just got busted by my sister."

Nick looked at me with trepidation. "Neither can I. Hey, I'm a rock star. This sort of thing's not supposed to happen. I deserve more respect."

He couldn't keep a straight face as he said that, and we both burst out laughing again. Quietly that time, both of us doing our best to keep the noise down.

I had a few sips of wine which somehow cleared my head a little, and something struck me as strange.

I turned to Nick. "Surely, Scarlett would have seen your car out front."

"No."

"What do you mean 'no'?" I shook my head. "Your place is miles away, way too far for you to have walked, and you don't walk anywhere if you can help it."

"I parked around the corner."

"Why?"

"Because I didn't think you'd want Scarlett to know I was here."

I didn't, yet I was sure she'd somehow worked it out. I wasn't ready to talk to Scarlett about Nick, and that meant I wasn't ready to talk to anybody. She'd give me some time. Not a lot, because whatever she truly thought, she'd come out with it sooner or later.

I kissed him on the nose. "You are way too sneaky, Nick Steel."

"Also, it would have ruined the surprise if you'd heard my car pull up."

I whacked him on the chest. "It wasn't a surprise. It was … an intrusion."

He raised his eyebrows. "Is this the way you treat intruders?"

Sitting up straight, I folded my arms. "You invaded my home, and I tried my best to fight you off."

He grinned. "Oh yeah, you fought really hard."

"Well, you'll have to leave the way you came in."

"Through the window?"

"Yeah but only because your butt will look so cute as you're climbing out."

"Who says I have to leave?"

Serious now, I lowered my voice. "You can't stay the night. You have to go eventually."

I couldn't lead Nick on and I couldn't do that to Thomas either. I also couldn't bear to go through that again with Nick.

He nodded. "Okay."

It wasn't okay. I saw it in his eyes. This was taking every ounce of patience he had. And I was grateful. He didn't tell me this was his house, didn't tell me Thomas was his son too, didn't try to get one over on me.

Maybe I'd underestimated him, and he was changing. He'd said he trusted me.

Problem was, I didn't trust myself.

CHAPTER TWELVE

Nick

It had started off as a friendly beer. Two friendly beers. I wasn't feeling quite so friendly now.

Austin was sitting next to me at the bar—my bar—because I'd invited him, mistakenly thinking this might be a casual meeting on my terms.

It wasn't that unusual being in a bar in the middle of the day. It reminded me of being on tour when we'd turn up someplace and have time to kill before the sound check. The four of us might have a beer, play some pool, chill for a bit, because there'd be nothing else to do. Playing gigs was a huge high. Unfortunately, there was a lot of waiting around that went with it.

Yet somehow now that we weren't touring, it didn't feel quite right being in a bar during the day, even though it had always felt fine with the band. We'd be working nights, traveling to the next gig during the day, and our lives had been so out of whack with the rest of society. So it'd made sense for us to have a drink while the rest of the world was doing their nine-to-five.

Right now, a lot of things didn't feel right. We'd just

had a long talk about architecture and bar design. Followed by something else.

I dropped my head into one hand. "You know I asked you here because you're an architect. Or that's what you were before the band took off. You've got the degree, a few years of work under your belt. And you've spent a lot of time in bars so I figured, hey, this guy might be able to help me out."

"Maybe I can."

I drank some beer. "Maybe you can leave."

He didn't budge.

Frustration simmered inside me. It wasn't that I didn't get where he was coming from because I did. Austin had always been the odd one out. Never intentionally. It was just the way things had worked out. And it wasn't just because of the quiff and the rockabilly clothes and the musical differences.

Lachie and Cooper and I had gone to school together. There was only a year between me and the two of them because I skipped a year in elementary school. I still wasn't sure how that had happened because I'd been bright but not exactly a genius. I'd always suspected Dad had paid someone off so Mom could brag about how clever her little boy was.

Austin had always been a big brother figure to us, the sensible one, the one who set us up with a manager and helped put us on the path to success. He'd also been the one most reluctant to give up his old life when we'd had to hit the road more seriously. I could see why now. Because he had the most to lose, not that I'd seen it then.

But that wasn't what was going on at the moment. That was something in a different league. Bombshell material. And it affected all of us.

"It doesn't have to be this way," he said.

"Yeah, it does. Do you have any idea how bad your timing is?"

I clenched my jaw, holding back the anger burning in my stomach. My life felt like a crumbling building with another piece of masonry that'd just fallen off and landed on the ground with a crash.

I sucked in a deep breath. The old Nick would have exploded, but I wasn't that person anymore. The new Nick wasn't going to lose his shit because he was a changed man.

"I feel for Lachie and his dad," Austin said. "I feel for Cooper, really I do."

We'd come back to town so Lachie could be with his father while he was getting treatment. While Cooper was getting his act together too because he had bigger problems than the rest of us. Man, our band had so many problems it wasn't funny, and now Austin was giving us the biggest shake-up ever, though maybe not as huge as Coops.

I knocked back a mouthful of beer. "I'm pissed, dude. I'm not gonna hide it."

"The plan was always to stay in town for six months, then see what happens. No reason that plan has to change. It means there's some time."

I shook my head in despair. "One thing's for sure. We'd better work out what the hell we're doing before The Flats."

We'd been hanging out to play at Frankston's big music festival. Or I thought we all had. That was the problem when you had four guys who all wanted something slightly different and there was one band.

Right now, the band was only one of the things on my mind. There was also the bar, Lily, Thomas, my parents, the list went on.

And the bar was the reason I'd asked Austin to meet me here. Because I'd thought Austin could help with some design direction for The Swamp, maybe with a concept or an actual architectural plan.

Now I wasn't sure what I thought because that was a huge project, too big for me to undertake on my own. Instead, it was back to square one.

I couldn't back down, though. I'd bought the bar and if I was going to do it, I was going to do it right. I had to stop fucking around and take decisive action.

No wonder they called this place The Swamp. That was how I felt now. Swamped. And I'd barely started.

"I can't talk to you right now, Austin."

So calm. No, I was trying to be, but I wasn't, not on the inside where fury was rolling around in my stomach, ready to spew forth at any minute.

Austin got up. "We can talk later."

Would we? I couldn't hold back any longer.

I waved him off. "Get the fuck out of here, dude."

Which was much better than a lot of other things I could have come out with. Now I was pissed at myself too because, as hard as I tried, I hadn't been able to keep my cool.

I didn't turn to say goodbye as Austin left. I knocked back what was left of my beer. It barely touched the sides. I was going to need something stronger to take the edge off things.

Tara, my hard-ass bartender, stood at the other end of

the bar wiping down the bar top and cleaning some imaginary grime off of something else. She took way too much pride in this place.

The woman must have had ESP because she came right over, and I asked for a bourbon with a beer chaser. She nodded and served me. Very obedient, which wasn't like her at all.

The bourbon burned the back of my throat and then the beer soothed it.

There weren't many people around in the middle of the day, just a few tourists down the back and a couple of old guys at the other end of the bar who looked like they'd spent way too much time here. Barflies. But they didn't look anywhere near as glamorous as Mickey Rourke in the movie.

I called Tara over, signaling that I'd like another drink, only for her upper lip to curl to a sneer. That was more like the Tara I knew.

Her hair was in some fifties style with a red scarf knotted at the top so I couldn't even see the purple streak in her hair. She was wearing a red-checkered shirt tied at the waist that matched her red lipstick.

Leaning over the bar, she raised one finely arched brow. "You sure? Haven't you had enough?"

It wasn't so much what she said as the way she said it. Sometimes I didn't know where she got off with that attitude.

"One of each," I said.

She hesitated, then thought better of it and poured the drinks. This was my bar, my rules, and we were doing this my way. I knocked back the bourbon, feeling it settle in my stomach. It wasn't enough though, not nearly enough.

I probably shouldn't have another drink, but what did I care? I shouldn't have told Austin to fuck off either. Yet another person to apologize to.

I looked up. Tara was still there. Giving me The Look.

"You need to up your game." She didn't raise her voice, kept her cool.

I kept mine for the time being too. "Why's that?"

"A bar with a drunk owner is going to lose a lot of money."

I shrugged. "So what? I've got a lot of money."

"Sixty-five hundred bars go out of business in this country each year."

"Huh? Where'd that come from?"

"Haven't you watched *Bar Rescue*?" I looked at her blankly so she added. "The TV show where they go to a failing bar, give the place an overhaul and the owners a lesson in how to run a bar."

"Can't say I have." I gulped back some beer, concentrating so I didn't slur my words. "I've been too busy making records and playing gigs."

"You're good at that." She nodded toward the band room. "I love The Merchants. Always have, ever since I first saw you guys play in that room over there back when I used to come in with my fake ID."

Maybe we were getting somewhere after all. "Thank you."

"You can make this place come to life again. Doesn't matter that there are other cities where rock 'n' roll is dead, we've still got a thriving band scene here. Up-and-coming bands, big bands like yours, all kinds of creative stuff is happening. You could be giving some young musicians the same chance you had back in the day. And you could make some money while you're at it."

"That'd be nice."

"But it won't just magically take place all on its own. You've got to stop drinking. You need to get your shit together."

What the hell? I couldn't believe she'd come out with that.

I stayed calm. "Don't you think you should be more careful?"

The look on her face said she wasn't going to take any shit from me, as if she'd forgotten the crap she'd just dished out.

My eyes narrowed. "Aren't you afraid of losing your job?"

"No, I'm trying to make sure I've still got a job."

I scowled. "What the fuck are you talking about now?"

"You can't have a bar with a drunken owner." She shook her head. "It doesn't work. The place is only going to lose money and go downhill. If the bar goes under, I won't have a job."

What she was saying made sense, except I wasn't a drunk. That couldn't be what she was getting at. Sure, I might've been drunk right now but that was only temporary.

I opened my mouth to argue, then saw Tara's lips had parted, a warning look on her face. Something was up. She shifted her gaze to something behind me.

I glanced around. Not something. *Someone.*

Lily. I froze. I hadn't forgotten about her, not exactly. I'd forgotten the time, not that that was going to be much help to me right now.

My heart was racing in an instant, perspiration beading

on my forehead. Fear skittered along my nerve endings, actual fear, because I'd made a big mistake.

I stood and gave Lily a hug and kissed her on the mouth. She didn't flinch, not exactly, but she gave me The Look, as if these two women had been colluding. If Lily hadn't already seen the empty glasses on the bar, she could no doubt smell the beer and bourbon. She could probably tell I'd been drinking just from seeing the back of my head as she walked in.

"I'll get you some water," Tara said and poured two glasses.

I sat down at the bar. "Thanks."

Tara leaned closer and whispered, "Play it nice or she'll throw it in your face."

I laughed because she couldn't possibly be serious, then glanced at Lily, saw her expression, and thought maybe my bartender knew exactly what she was talking about. She headed to the other side of the bar to serve an old guy who'd signaled her, leaving me with Lily.

She raised her eyebrows, her lips tight. "Hard day?"

"You could say that. Take a seat."

She edged onto the barstool beside me.

"How's Thomas doing today?" I asked. "Was he excited about Granny taking him to the zoo?"

"Very." She smiled, couldn't help herself. "He thinks a special outing with just the two of them is very grown up."

"It is."

"And it gave me a few hours for myself." Her shoulders dropped. So did her smile. "I thought you wanted to spend some time together, just the two of us."

"I do."

"You're drunk, Nick."

"Something came up. Sorry, this isn't how I planned things."

She sipped her water, ignoring me.

I hated being ignored. "What, Lily?"

"Something always comes up."

"Austin came by. It was meant to be a business meeting."

She stared down at the empty glasses in front of me. "A business meeting?"

"About the bar, not the band."

I couldn't tell her what Austin had said, not now. It was eating away at me, anger building inside, anger that I had to hold back because that was supposed to be my time with Lily, and I'd gotten off to a bad start.

I looked around. "This place needs a makeover. Doesn't take a genius to work that out, but it does take an expert who knows what he's doing."

"Professional advice, you mean?"

"Yeah."

"You could ask Scarlett. She's an interior architect, don't forget."

"Doesn't she do houses?"

"She does a lot of things."

"I need someone who knows bars and hospitality, who knows the business, a seasoned professional."

Lily's dark eyes turned to steel. "I hope you don't think all she does is scatter a few cushions and choose the paint colors. Because her job entails a lot more than that."

Shit, my words had come out all wrong. I hadn't meant to insult her. Hell, I liked Scarlett. Always had. I just thought speaking to an architect rather than an interior architect would be a better place to start.

Lily clenched her jaw. "It's the middle of the day, Nick, and you're pissed. I could smell it on you as soon as I walked in. That wasn't a business meeting. It was a joke."

"I've had a couple of beers. I'm not drunk. There's a difference."

Lily's words echoed my father's, words that still ate away at me, that sent a knife stabbing though my chest. He'd pointed out that I didn't have a business plan, just some crazy ideas, and I didn't want him to be right about me. He'd pointed out a lot more than that too. Thought I was a loser, an alcoholic, a failure.

I wasn't any of the things my father thought I was.

Lily slid off her barstool. "Maybe I should get going. Clearly you've got more important things to do."

I grabbed her arm. "Lily, you're the most important thing to me, you and Thomas."

"Sometimes you don't act like it."

"It's the truth."

She shook me off. "I need someone I can rely on, someone who doesn't miss a beat, someone who'll be there. It's just as well I've got my mom and my family."

"You've got me too, Lily."

"No, I don't, Nick. Not like this."

For a moment, I saw myself through her eyes. A guy who played in a band who was drunk in the middle of the day.

She had it wrong. That wasn't who I was.

Lily gave me a look like she'd never have me, a look that broke my heart because I'd come such a long way, and this was only one small slip-up. Sometimes she forgot I had a heart too. And it was all hers.

"You've got a drinking problem," she said.

I'd seen a lot of addicts. We'd even had one in the band. I wasn't an alcoholic, just a guy who liked to drink, and she should know that.

So I told it like it was. "I've got a lot of problems, and drinking is not one of them."

Her eyes were two warnings.

I drank my glass of water and stood. "I'll stop drinking right now if you like."

"Yep."

She didn't believe me.

"Can I see you later?" I asked.

"No, I'm going out tonight, Nick. You wouldn't like it. It's alcohol-free, not your style. I go to Dancing in the Dark because I'm too uptight to dance in front of anyone else, as you've pointed out to me before."

"I never said that, Lily." I was feeling suddenly sober. "I was teasing you, that's all."

"Yeah, well you made it feel serious."

Now it was my fault?

She pursed her lips. "See you later."

I let her leave and dropped my head into my hands. I shouldn't have had a few drinks this afternoon, but not everything in the world was my fault.

Damn it, so much for trying to turn over a new leaf. I sucked in a deep breath, looked around the bar. My bar. I was the owner, and I was taking control.

The leaf was turned. From now on, there'd be no more fucking up. I was doing this right.

CHAPTER THIRTEEN

Lily

It was so good to have some 'me' time, except that wasn't what I wanted. Before Nick had come back to town, I'd had my act together, my routines, my job, my time with Thomas. Now I didn't know what I wanted anymore.

Though I wouldn't have described myself as calm, I'd cooled down a lot since leaving the bar this afternoon and had even started having doubts. Maybe Nick had only had one or two drinks. Maybe he wasn't that drunk, and I'd overreacted. Maybe I was exactly the sort of accusing, demanding, unreasonable woman he didn't want in his life.

Or maybe I'd been right in the first place, and he was a prick. Damn it, I hated the way he made me feel.

Memories of what we were like together in my bedroom came tumbling back, and all those doubts dissolved because that couldn't possibly have been just sex to him. It was more. I knew it was.

I'd made an effort to get dressed up even though we were going to be in the dark, and I had chosen a cute skirt and stay-up stockings in a cool checked pattern. I liked them and didn't care whether they were in fashion or not.

I paid the cover charge, a bargain at five bucks, even for me. The Scout Hall was a cool, old building, just a big room with a stage at the front, wooden floorboards, and white walls. There were no Boy Scouts here tonight, however, only dancers. Not that I was a dancer, just someone who liked to dance.

As I walked through the door into the main hall, I saw Amber signaling to me from the front of the room, waving like a crazy idiot which was one of the reasons I liked her. I headed straight down the front and gave her a high five when I got there.

Another thing I liked was the range of characters in this place, young people and old, short and tall, fat and thin. It was just a bunch of people who were out to have fun and maybe get a bit of exercise.

"You ready?" I asked.

"As I'll ever be." Amber lifted a foot onto one of the chairs lining the wall, straightened her leg, and leaned forward from the hips.

"You're stretching?"

"I was a bit sore after last time."

I motioned to the opposite side of the room. "I thought you might be turning pro."

The dancers on the other side looked like actual dancers, unlike everyone else in the room. They stretched before each session, some of them so flexible I'd even seen them do the splits. Amber and I had long suspected they took this much more seriously than we did.

"Pro? Not likely." She swapped legs. "See, that's the exact reason this stuff has to happen in the dark."

"So we don't look bad."

"Exactly."

I smiled, tossing my hair back. "Anyway, we look fantastic!"

"Absolutely."

I turned to the DJ booth at the front and tried to work out who was on tonight. Each DJ did their own thing which was not always 'my' thing, but I tried to get into the music no matter what. For instance, I wasn't exactly Hip-Hop Gal but the last time I was here, I'd gotten into the zone with the likes of Kendrick Lamar, Chance the Rapper, and Drake. Boy, had he come a long way since Degrassi! And I'd loved it.

Amber was frowning. "You didn't tell me…"

"Huh?" I turned toward the entrance where she was looking. "Tell you what?"

"Oh, um, it's DJ Dolomite tonight. Isn't that great?"

"So why were you looking at the door?"

She grabbed my arm, her eyes wide. "That means we're getting a hard rock mix, my favorite. I couldn't get into the music last time."

"Really? I loved it."

"Oh no, hard rock is the way to go. Much better. I always thought you were more of a rock chick."

I tilted my head. "Are you feeling okay tonight, Amber?"

"Oh, you know, I just want to get started."

At that moment, the lights went down.

I squeezed her hand. "What timing."

They always waited a few seconds before starting the music so our eyes could adjust to the dark and we didn't bump into each other. Eventually, I could see movement and shapes, and I took a deep breath while I waited.

The guitar riff from the Black Rebel Motorcycle Club

blared through the sound system, resonating through the room. I didn't know which song, and it didn't matter because it was BRMC.

I started to move. The music seeped into me. I felt it. And I let rip. I danced the way I wanted to dance. I danced the same way I sang in the shower. Like I didn't care.

Foo Fighters, The Killers, Wolf Alice, I heard some of my favorites. The DJ even played The Escape Artists, a new band from right here in Frankston, and I was thrilled to be part of this town.

I was a teenager again. As the night went on, I'd become a sweaty mess, and I'd keep dancing like no one was watching. Because they weren't. It was only me and the music, and I could do what I wanted.

Not for a minute did I feel alone, though. I was somehow still interacting with these people. There was an energy that pervaded us, that we shared and all understood. I was part of something.

Then renewed vigor surged through me as DJ Dolomite played The Merchants of Menace. I'd known he would. You couldn't have rock 'n' roll in Frankston without The Merchants. *Love Like Electricity*. My favorite song. Or one of them. I had so many favorites.

That was when I heard it. Nick's voice sailing over the top of the music. His actual voice, not the record.

Nick. He was here.

I kept moving, slower than before. My eyes were wide open, searching the room, even though I could only see shapes. Somehow, I knew that if he was here, he'd find me. I felt his presence, sensed him closing in, getting nearer.

His voice became louder. Behind me. I turned. Was he

there? Was I imagining things?

I kept dancing, moving around, searching aimlessly. I was suddenly disoriented, unsure of my bearings. Breathless, I wondered if I should leave.

Strong hands slid onto my waist. He was behind me. It was him, I knew it. Every nerve ending in my body alight, I let out a long moan; I couldn't help myself.

Nick sidled closer but kept his hands where they were. My breath caught in my throat. I kept dancing, pretending, He was moving behind me. Closer. Sliding his body against mine.

"Lily." A whisper in my ear, his breath moist. "My beautiful Lily."

I arched my neck, melting against his touch. My insides were molten, on fire, burning, ready to explode. How did he do that to me?

He circled around to the front of me, stood close, and took my hands in his.

The song finished. I didn't move.

Some guy nearby raised his voice. "Ugh, that dude can't even sing."

We both laughed. If only that person had any idea.

As the next song started, Nick whispered something to me. I didn't quite catch it. He pulled me through the crowd, weaving his way slowly through the moving shapes in front of us, and pulled open the velvet curtain into the front entry.

The lights here had been dimmed.

But the fire inside me was blazing.

CHAPTER FOURTEEN

Nick

This wasn't the Lily I knew and yet it was. This was the shy flower from inside the scout hall who was dancing in the dark, and it was a hot little hellcat who couldn't get her hands off me. Mine, all mine.

God only knew I wanted her hands on me, everywhere. I wanted all of her engulfing me. And I wanted it now.

Though I was the one who'd led her out of the hall, she pushed past me, yanked my hand until we were out the door and around the corner, down the side of the building. It was dark. Cold. We were in an alley. Music blaring from inside.

And there was only me and Lily.

She pushed me up against the wall. Reverberations from the drum beat resonated through my body. A cat shrieked in the distance. Lily pulled my head down and pressed her mouth against mine in a kiss that was hot, hungry, and instant.

Her hands were on my waist, lifting my shirt. There was a shock of cold air on my stomach, then her warm hands reaching, fumbling, and a magic moment of bliss as her hands engulfed my erection.

No waiting, no foreplay, no nothing. That was exactly what I wanted. Lily was everything I wanted.

Wrapping my arms around her, I spun her around, pushing her up against the wall. I lifted her top. She gasped. It must've been from the cold. I pulled down the cups of her bra to take one nipple into my mouth, then the other. Those breasts fit so perfectly into my hands, and I wanted to devour them, knead them, hold them forever.

Lily moaned, such a wonderful sound, then pulled me closer. She reached for my cock again, and I knew neither of us was going to be able to wait. I yanked down my jeans to below my butt. Just low enough. I couldn't waste any time. My erection sprung out of my pants. I'd never been so ready in all my life.

She pulled her skirt up over her hips and got rid of her panties. I didn't even know how she did it. The sight of her nakedness drove me wild. Man, I remembered that from before. She used to wear these stay-up pantyhose that finished around those creamy white thighs and drove me crazy, made me want more. She was wearing them now. Stockings, bare skin, a patch of pubic hair. And hiding in there was the place I wanted to be.

I lifted her higher so she could wrap her legs around me, then entered the wonderful warmth of her and moaned. Lily gasped, her breaths short and fast, her fingers digging into my back. She was with me all the way, moving against me until she shrieked with ultimate pleasure. It tipped me over the edge, my orgasm rocketing through me.

She was still pressed up against the wall. I held her

close. I didn't want to let her go. We were both panting, spent, exhausted. Gently lowering her to the ground, I kissed her on the mouth, and pressed little kisses to her cheeks, her forehead, then nuzzled into her neck.

I could've stayed here all night, except it was fucking freezing out. But I could've stayed with Lily all night for sure. If she'd have me. That was the big question.

My pulse was still high, my heart swelling so much my chest hurt. She was causing me actual pain, and I was loving every minute of it. That was how powerful this thing inside me was.

"I love you," I whispered the words in her ear, then pulled back.

Her eyes were misty, her skin glowing, as her lips curled to a shy smile. My lovely Lily. Always holding back.

Maybe my eyes were a little misty too as some strange power pervaded the rest of my body, spreading outward from my heart, settling in my stomach, sinking deep into my bones.

She was part of me. I didn't ever want to lose her; I couldn't bear the thought.

It was an emotion and it was a realization too and nothing to do with the sex. It was Lily I loved. It'd always been her. I'd just been too stupid to see it.

CHAPTER FIFTEEN

Lily

How could I be so sensible and matter of fact when Nick and I were so insane when we were together? How could I put on a new dress and makeup and go out to dinner with people from work when all I wanted to do was stay home with my two favorite boys?

And maybe have wild, passionate sex with Nick. There was that too. Then again, there was no 'maybe' about it. Still, we could get onto that after I got back because no way was I staying out late when I had dessert waiting for me at home.

Meanwhile, I'd pretend to be a normal, fully functioning member of society, a mother, a working woman, a girlfriend. Was that what I was? I didn't feel like a girlfriend. I felt like something else.

I was happy for other reasons too. I'd sent off my application to Frankston College. I didn't have a plan on how I'd earn money, study full-time, and look after Thomas, and right now I didn't care. I'd taken the first step, and that was all that mattered.

Leaning in the doorway of the bathroom, life had

never looked better. Thomas was splashing around in the bath with a red toy garden trowel of all things, singing a song he'd made up and blowing raspberries. Sometimes I wondered what went through his little head and sometimes he was so adorable it made my heart ache.

Nick was sitting on the blue stool, looking about as sexy as any man could possibly look with his knees up high on a child's stool, his phone on the floor on the other side of him. I bit my lip to stop myself from asking why he'd brought it in here because that'd only be nagging.

Thomas moved through the water, making waves, probably with some game in mind. Kneeling, he started to lever himself up, but Nick grabbed his arm and shook his head.

"No standing in the bath!" My heart clenched. I was drowning, water up my nose, no air, lungs burning. *Not Thomas. Not him too.*

"But Mommy, I was just–"

Nick gave him a stern look. "You were just sitting down, weren't you?"

My hand pressed against my chest, I stopped myself from interfering.

"Okay." Thomas picked up the toy trowel again, scooped up some water and tipped it out, not disturbed by any of that.

And I could breathe again.

Sometimes I was okay around water, and at other times I was a nine-year-old kid with my head held underwater. I forced myself to calm down and waited a few minutes until my pulse had slowed. I told myself it was just a phobia and that nothing bad had happened.

I tried to focus on the good things in my life which

wasn't so hard because they were right in front of me. Thomas, a happy, healthy little boy. And Nick…

Last night, he'd told me he loved me. My breath caught in my throat. My heart stopped, then started again. I couldn't believe how emotional I was getting tonight.

Years ago, we'd spoken those words to each other, back when we'd been young and in love. Nick wouldn't have said he loved me if he didn't. He wasn't that sort of guy.

Which meant only one thing. I took a long, slow breath. I breathed him in, my chest flooding with warmth, my entire being filling with joy. This was everything I'd ever wanted it. Something so special, I'd barely even dared to dream it. And later tonight, I'd tell him exactly how I felt about him.

"It's lovely seeing the two of you together like this." I was stating the obvious.

Thomas looked up. "But Mommy, you've seen me in my bath lots of times."

I nodded. "Yes, I have, pumpkin."

"I haven't done this a lot of times, though," Nick said. "Not fair."

He pulled a face and made Thomas giggle.

I continued with the theme of stating the obvious. "It's nice having you around."

In so many ways. It was finally starting to feel like we were a family. Scarlett was family, but that was different. She'd gone out tonight. She'd been going out a lot lately, and that was fine. It was also a huge relief not to have to worry about a babysitter for a change because Nick was here.

"I've got my phone with me," I said. "I'll check it from

131

time to time. The restaurant is bound to be noisy so I won't hear it."

"No problem." Nick looked up at me, a sparkle in his eye. "You won't be late, will you?"

I smiled. "No, I won't."

Maybe I should stay home after all. I could text to say I couldn't make it tonight. No, I was being ridiculous. I still needed some balance in my life. It was only dinner, after all, and by the time I got back, Thomas would be tucked up in bed and Nick would be…

By the sound of it, Nick would be ready. My heart swooned all over again.

I leaned over and kissed him on the mouth, then realized what I'd done because this wasn't something I did in front of Thomas. I'd been so strict with myself, never wanting to mislead him in that way. I glanced across at my son talking softly to himself, then looked into the cool blue of Nick's eyes and melted all over again.

Screw being strict. My chest heaving, I pressed my lips against his and held them there in a kiss that left no doubt. Thomas might not have sensed what this meant but Nick would. As I pulled away, he gave me a lingering look.

"Hey, what about me?" Thomas yelled.

I leaned closer. "I've got lipstick on so I'll have to be careful."

He waved me off. "No yukky lipstick for me."

I blew him a kiss instead, and he did the same. I pretended to catch the kiss on my cheek which made him laugh, the most beautiful sound in the world. And as I stood, I brushed my hand against Nick's shoulder, a loving touch to tell him how much this meant to me.

"Hey," Thomas said. "You kissed Daddy on the mouth."

I nodded. "I know."

Thomas' eyes narrowed. "I saw you."

"And you might see it again, pumpkin."

Thomas smiled. Nick too. In fact, Nick was grinning from ear to ear. Like me.

And it was going to stay that way.

CHAPTER SIXTEEN

Nick

I had that Neil Armstrong feeling again. One small step, one small kiss, one big step for mankind.

Except it hadn't been me who'd taken the step. It'd been Lily, and that was what made it so wonderful. She'd meant it too. So many small steps—and big ones too— leading up to this moment.

Things had changed between the two of us big time. We were having sex, but it was so much more because there was a big difference between having sex and making love. Except for last time. That'd been different. If you were in an alleyway, it was sex. That was part of the deal. And that had been absolutely amazing, whichever way I looked at it.

"Vroom, vroom."

Thomas concentrated on maneuvering his boat through the water. His hair was wet, his light-brown curls sagging, giving him a drowned rat look. Super cute.

"Hey," I said. "That's not the sound boats make."

"This one does," he said with great confidence.

I'd missed out on so much. I'd been such a prick; there

was no point mincing my words. After Lily and I had broken up, there'd been a lot of girls, too many to count, and that hadn't necessarily been such a good thing even if it'd seemed like a good idea at the time.

None of it compared with this, with the simple beauty of giving my child his bath, with the gentleness and certainty of Lily's kiss, with the knowledge that she'd be back later, and we'd have tonight and tomorrow and the day after that.

I was twenty-four now and could see this as clear as day. I hadn't been able see it when I was twenty. Hadn't been able to see past my dick. And maybe my ego.

"Am I being funny, Daddy?"

"I like watching you, that's all."

I was grinning from the tips of my toes to the top of my head because life couldn't have been better. Thomas thought I was smiling because of what he was doing, and he was partly right. He was a gorgeous kid. My son. And I was finally being a father.

Which made us a family.

My phone rang. I glanced down. Lachie's name flashed on the screen. Damn it, did I want to talk to him? My stomach sank at the thought because this was going to be a crappy conversation, but it was better to get it out of the way sooner rather than later.

I picked up the phone. "Yo, Lachie."

Thomas was knocking around in the bath with his trowel. I couldn't figure out why he liked that thing so much. Meanwhile, Lachie was in my ear about Austin, as I knew he would be. I couldn't blame him. We had a lot to talk about.

I opened my mouth to speak and got a mouthful of

bathwater thanks to Thomas' exuberant splashing around.

He covered his mouth and giggled. "Sorry, Daddy."

Spluttering, I grabbed the hand towel and wiped my face.

"What's up, man?" Lachie said through the phone.

"Hang on, Thomas just splashed me."

That might not have sounded very rock 'n' roll, and I didn't care. This was who I was now. I was also kind of wet.

Getting to my feet, I shifted to the doorway so I could lean against the frame in relative comfort and dryness. Just as I expected, the conversation was a long one. There was no point trying to talk sense into Lachie or reason with him when all he wanted to do was talk and get this off his chest. Fair enough. I let him go for it.

I was thinking Thomas' bath must've been getting cold, not that he seemed to notice. He was way too busy with his boat and his trowel. He got noisier, like he was making the sounds of a whole construction team, his little brow furrowing in concentration.

Turning away, I pressed a finger to my free ear, cut in, and told Lachie I had to go. He could like it or not, lump it or leave it.

I turned back to Thomas. Standing in his bath. Walking, knees high.

"Look at me, I'm a running man."

"Nooooo."

He slipped and slid back. It happened in slow motion. The phone dropped from my hand. I leaped forward. He was falling. I reached for him. Not quick enough. His head hit the back of the bath. A horrible thud.

His face was underwater. I grabbed him under his

arms and pulled him up.

"Thomas, Thomas."

His head hung forward. He was supposed to splutter, cry, scream, something, anything.

Instead, there was nothing.

Panic shot through me like a switch that'd been flicked. I was panting, my heart racing, muscles twitching.

I lifted him out of the bath. Limp. Not moving. Unconscious. Both of us drenched, I grabbed a towel and wrapped it over him as best I could.

Fear sliced through my heart like a knife, so sharp I was in pain. I hurt like I'd never hurt before.

Shit, what to do? I couldn't think straight. I also couldn't let myself be paralyzed by fear. He needed me.

I slid my hand between us and pressed it against his little chest. His heart was pumping. He was breathing. Thank God, he was breathing. My relief didn't last long. I looked down at him slumped against my chest, his eyes half-open, his jaw slack, and the pain in my heart deepened.

I forced myself to think. The phone. 911. Paramedics. No, I'd take him to Frankston General myself. It'd be quicker if I drove.

Bending over, I swept my phone from the floor and headed for the kitchen table where I'd left my keys, then straight out of the front door to my car.

Thomas... Thomas... My beautiful boy.

What had I done? I'd have to call Lily. Dear God, how was I ever going to explain? And Thomas. Please let him be okay.

CHAPTER SEVENTEEN

Lily

The phone call every parent dreaded, except I'd never thought it would be me. Never thought it would happen this way.

My gut clenched into a knot as I gazed at my baby's sleeping face. Thomas' eyes were closed, his skin so pale and soft, his cheeks like little pillows. It didn't matter that he was four years old. He'd always be my baby. My eyes filled with tears at the thought of how much I could have lost.

I'd rather it'd been me, damn it. If I had to choose between my life and his, I wouldn't give it a second thought. I'd throw myself in front of a train to save him.

I swallowed back the tears and looked around the room while I tried to pull myself together. Two walls were painted pale pink and two were blue, as if the designers had been hedging their bets. The sides were pulled up on the hospital bed, standard practice perhaps. The wall behind Thomas was covered with rolled up tubing, screens and monitors, and assorted other medical equipment.

I didn't look at Nick sitting in the chair beside me.

Thomas was okay. As best they could make out, he'd been unconscious for a few minutes after slipping in the bath and landing on his head and now had a concussion. Normally, they sent kids home after something like this, but the doctors were keeping him overnight for observation because his symptoms were so extreme. He'd been crying from the pain of a headache, throwing up from the nausea, and had been so confused that nothing he said made sense. All of which was normal after head trauma, apparently. It was the combination of factors that wasn't so good.

Still, he'd be fine and that was the main thing. That was what I told myself. It didn't work. My heart twisted, anger surging in my stomach. Nick should have had his eye on him. Damn it, this should never have happened.

I took a deep breath and forced myself to calm down because my head was a mess, and I needed to get the facts clear first.

"Do you want to tell me exactly what happened?"

Nick nodded and went through the story step by step. He kept his voice down so as not to wake Thomas, but the poor kid was sleeping so soundly it'd take a bomb to wake him.

We took it slow, and I asked a couple of questions. Nick spoke, and I knew. He hadn't been looking after him properly.

It was almost as if I'd had a sixth sense too. Mother's intuition perhaps. Or maybe it was simply because I knew Nick.

Either way, even before I'd picked up the phone, I'd known something was wrong. Earlier this evening, I hadn't been able to check my phone until I'd parked outside the restaurant because I never fiddled with my phone while I was driving, no matter what.

After that, I'd listened to Nick's message twice. The first time all I'd heard was 'Thomas' and 'hospital.' And the tremor in Nick's voice. I'd heard that loud and clear. That same fear coursed through me.

I dropped my head into my hands and tried to stop myself from shaking.

"Lily, I was standing in the doorway," Nick said.

I clenched my teeth and turned to him. "You weren't watching him."

"I was right there when it happened."

"You were on the phone. You had your back to him. You already told me." I spat the words out. "So don't try and tell me you had your eye on him the whole time."

"I turned away for a second. Only a second."

"And that was all it took."

Lips thin, he didn't say anything. If he was mad, so was I.

I clenched my fists to stop myself from losing it completely. Too many competing feelings, too much to handle. Fury was still rolling in my stomach, and the initial shock hadn't left me. That despair had sunk deep into my bones, and I couldn't shake it.

Nick opened his mouth to speak, but I got in first. "Don't tell me to be reasonable."

I knew him too well because that was exactly what he was going to say.

He waited. "Do you have any idea how this feels for me?"

I didn't answer.

"There's no point trying to make me feel worse than I

already do. I'm the one who did bad, and I know just how much I have to feel guilty about. He's my son too."

"I know you love him…" My voice trailed off.

"But what? I'm not good enough? I can't take care of him?"

"I didn't say that."

"It's what you were thinking. Don't deny it."

Neither of us said anything. We sat there, our silence a wall between us until minutes passed and Nick spoke.

"Lily, I should've been there, and I'm sorry. Believe me, I couldn't be more sorry. But what I did … a lot of other people would have done it too. Any other parent in my position would have thought nothing of stepping a few feet away and turning around for a second."

I couldn't help the venom boiling inside me. "I. Don't. Care."

Nick hesitated. "You've got a problem with being around water."

"What? So I should get over it?"

"That's not what I'm getting at."

"I told you about having my head held underwater as a kid and not being able to breathe. Plenty of times."

"Y-yeah."

I raised my eyebrows. "And you weren't listening. Didn't take much notice. Maybe that's part of the problem too, Nick, that you brush me off."

A muscle in his jaw flinched. I'd hit a sore spot, and I was going to make him hurt.

"I always thought it would be the booze that was the final straw," I said through my teeth. "I never thought it would be something like this."

I couldn't believe the words coming from my mouth,

the anger inside me, the fear still thrumming through my body.

He didn't say anything. I let him simmer in his pain. It should have felt good to have come out with that. Instead, the weight of my vengeance hung over me like a shroud.

Despite everything, Nick's patience amazed me. He took Thomas' little hand into his and waited. He walked to the window, lifted the blinds, and stared into nothingness, then came back to his seat again and leaned forward, his arms resting on his thighs.

Eventually he said, "There are two chairs. I'd like to stay here tonight too."

I looked across at him, my lower lip trembling because I wanted Nick so badly and yet I couldn't bear to have him around.

"You should go," I said.

He stared at his hands clasped in front of him, opened his mouth to speak, then thought better of it. He turned to me, pain etched in his features, his eyes glistening. Maybe this was too much for him too. I'd never seen him cry.

My throat suddenly tight, I was choked up, tears welling in my eyes in an instant, tears that hadn't fallen this evening because I'd been too scared.

Nick got up and looked down at his son. He smoothed down his lovely light-brown curls and kissed him on the cheek. "Love you, Thomas."

As Nick turned to me, so many emotions were surging inside me, I didn't know what to think or feel anymore. Tears were streaming down my cheeks, and I was about to start sobbing any second now.

He stepped behind my chair toward the door, then stopped. "I love you, Lily."

Then he left.

And my heart that had already been broken shattered into a thousand pieces.

CHAPTER EIGHTEEN

Nick

Five days had passed. It felt like five years.

Thomas had needed almost complete rest for the first couple of days after his accident, but it was extremely hard to keep a four-year-old boy calm. He'd been very confused for the first day, saying weird stuff, forgetting what he was doing, and had now somehow bounced back with renewed energy levels that were hard to keep in check.

Still, it wasn't safe for him to run around again or be in any situation where he might crash into something or bump his head. And I wasn't going to forget it.

After that first night at the hospital, Lily had agreed to let me visit Thomas—supervised visits, something that rankled—but I was taking what I could get. Lily had cooled down slightly since that night and had probably relented because it was blaringly obvious I'd have gotten my lawyer onto it right away. God only knew I felt bad enough about the whole thing as it was.

I'd been visiting Lily's place every day and coming up with all sorts of ideas for quiet play and non-active things to keep Thomas occupied. I was doing a good job of it too. Uno was the biggest hit ever which just went to show that sometimes the simplest things worked the best.

Lily had taken a few days off work but had to go back today. Reluctantly. She'd let me look after him today. Also reluctantly. My first unsupervised visit.

This morning, Thomas and I had built a blanket fort using the dining table at my place by covering it with a huge cloth, lining the floor with a comforter—for comfort—and bringing selected toys into our new hiding place. It was the perfect size for Thomas. Not so good for me. My back had been killing me afterwards.

After lunch, we'd read some books together, and I'd thought I could set him up with some cartoons on my laptop in the music room while I worked on a couple of songs. I'd thought wrong. There were way too many distractions in there for Thomas, and he was way too excited about having all this 'Daddy time.'

He snuck up to the Stratocaster on a stand in the corner, crouched down, looked up at me, then plucked a string.

I raised my eyebrows. "Thomas."

He got that sneaky look and did it again, but I couldn't be mad at him.

"Stay right there," I told him as I opened one door of the cupboard where I stored some other gear. I spun around and caught him moving, so he giggled, then froze in place. Turning back to the closet, I reached for the acoustic guitar which I thought might be a better starting point for someone Thomas' size.

"Do you think four is too young for your first guitar lesson?" I asked.

He jumped to his feet, his face lighting up. "Ooh, I'm big for four."

Yep, huge. It made me smile. I took Thomas to the

sofa in the living room where he'd be more comfortable and showed him how to hold the guitar. He started off very serious, hanging off my every word, tentative about strumming the strings.

It wasn't long until he'd written his first song, the words of which were shouted and repeated. Somehow, I doubted *I'm Playing Guitar* was going to be a hit. Then again, my first song hadn't been a hit either. Nope, it'd been a load of crap.

After he was done, Thomas handed the guitar back to me. "I was talking to Granny on the phone yesterday, and she doesn't know how to play Uno." He jumped off the sofa. "I know, maybe we can teach her."

"Not today. She had a big outing today with her friends."

That was one of the reasons Lily had seemed grateful I could step in and look after Thomas.

He tugged at my hand. "What about Baba?"

Lily's grandmother. "You want to visit Baba?"

"To teach her how to play Uno." His eyes sparkled. "Also Baba has really good candy."

Thomas kept nagging, and I wasn't sure what to do, so I texted Lily to check if it was okay. No way did I want to do anything to get her riled. After that, I phoned Baba who, not surprisingly, loved the idea of a little visitor.

When we turned up at her place, we headed straight for the backyard, and it turned out she had an ulterior motive—the tree that needed pruning, the one I'd forgotten about.

"No problem," I told her. There were a couple of dead branches on the oak, not so big that I'd need ropes and not so high that I couldn't get to them. "Where do you keep the saw?"

She pointed. "In the shed."

Thomas tugged at her hand and looked up at me. "Daddy, we'll be inside."

"Okay, you'll play nice and quietly, won't you?"

Baba nodded. "Lily, she already tell me about this concussion. We'll be nice and quiet."

"Yes, we will," Thomas said.

"Also you must be quiet because Dida is having an afternoon sleep," Baba added. "He needs his rest."

Thomas was very firm as he led her into the house because he wasn't shy around the people he loved.

Cutting through the two branches with the bow saw took a serious amount of elbow grease, but it felt good to be sitting up high and doing something physical.

I used to help the gardener out at home. The first time I'd done it was because I'd been a bored kid. After that, I'd done it because it gave my father the shits for me to be hanging with the hired help. It'd worked every time.

Cutting the branches into manageable lengths took even more work, but I wasn't going to leave the job half-done. I stacked the logs to one side because Baba had already told me she was giving them to someone for firewood.

I checked my phone when I was done, only to find a message from Lily saying she'd left work early and was at home. I could almost have pretended this was a normal communication between two parents. Almost. I texted her right back so she knew Thomas was safe and that we weren't quite ready to leave yet.

The back door creaked open. Baba was holding the door for Thomas who was carrying a tall glass of cold water out for me. Perfect timing.

Sweat was pouring off me, my tee shirt was smeared with dirt, and I couldn't have been happier about it. I knocked back the water and put the glass by the door.

Baba reached for my arm. "Thank you so much, Nick."

Thomas nodded proudly. "My daddy is very strong."

"So are you." I handed him the saw. "Do you think you could help me carry this to the shed?"

With a serious expression on his face, he 'helped' me and then wandered across to inspect the woodpile.

"Such a beaaauuutiful boy." Baba drew the word out, then added, "I'm so much smarter than my daughter or granddaughter."

I had no idea where this was going but I agreed anyway.

She nodded knowledgeably. "I married a younger man. Despite his dementia, he'll still be around for a long time."

"I didn't know Dida was younger than you."

"By four years. Sandra married a man who was ten years older than her, and he got sick. A heart attack."

"I know. I'm sorry."

She turned and glared at me. "And Lily found a man who ran away."

"I didn't run."

She waved me off. "You ran like Usain Bolt with his long legs."

My cue to leave.

"But you're not running now," she added. "And you did a good job with the tree. Thank you."

I opened my mouth to speak, then stopped. *You did a good job.* Such simple words yet they meant so much. My father had never said that to me, not even when I'd been a kid. He'd never said it when I'd gotten A's at school, so I'd stopped bothering. He hadn't said it when the first album had gone gold, then platinum. He'd never say it.

Maybe there were some things I should say to him too. Maybe it was time I said what I was thinking the same way Baba did because skirting around the truth wasn't getting me anywhere. And I was starting to see through the crap.

Thomas turned from the woodpile, ready to sprint across the yard.

"No running!"

"Sorry, I forgot." So obedient, he slowed down.

I met him in the middle of yard and ruffled his hair. "Might be time to take you home."

We wandered through the house to get the Uno cards, and Baba walked us to my car out front. Thomas gave her a big hug and a sloppy kiss, and by the look on her face, she couldn't get enough of him. Leaning across, she gave me a hug too, a big surprise.

"Drive careful," she said.

I smiled at her accent and grammar. The woman knew how to get her message across.

We made it to Lily's place in no time. I took Thomas' hand to stop him from hurtling up the front path and got another "Sorry" from him.

As soon as the front door opened, Thomas started telling Lily how he played at Baba's and beat her at Uno. A lot of times, apparently.

Lily beamed at him. "That's wonderful, pumpkin. You can go inside now."

Thomas scooted through while she stood in the doorway, the smile leaving her face as she turned to me. I remembered when I used to make her smile, when I could've reached across and tickled her, when my touch had put her in raptures.

Angst settled deep in my stomach, eating away at me because I couldn't bear for things to be this way between us. I wanted more, so much more.

She leaned against the door. "Thanks for looking after Thomas."

"You don't need to thank me. I'm his dad. I love every moment with him." Baba's words came back to me. "Did I do a good job?"

A pause. "I don't know yet. We'll have to wait and see."

Not the answer I was expecting, but it shouldn't have surprised me. I'd have to earn Lily's trust. In fact, that was exactly what I was doing even if she couldn't see it yet.

I turned away. "I have to go."

Which was true. I wanted to finish those songs I hadn't been able to work on today. They were in my head, and I needed to get them down. Also, I'd cancelled a band meeting, and we needed to reschedule.

There were other people I needed to speak to as well. My father, for one, because one way or another, I was going to tell him exactly what I thought.

And Austin. I shook my head as I walked down the front path. I may have told him to fuck off, but I still needed his help as a starting point with the bar at the very least.

So many things were going through my head.

I turned back when I reached the car. Lily had closed the door, no lingering looks, no second thoughts, not for her. It sent a pang through my chest. It didn't matter that I should've known better. I still kept hoping.

A lot of things were going through my heart too.

And all of them to do with Lily.

CHAPTER NINETEEN

Lily

No one had ever told me being a parent would hurt this much. People talked about the sleepless nights with babies and toddlers, and the difficulty of getting through the teenage years. I hadn't realized the pain, the agony, at the thought of losing your child.

I knew it now. Better not to dwell on it. If only I could get it out of my head. I had to stop being a control freak. After all, I had to let go sometime.

"Can I have a glass of milk, please, Mommy?"

Yep, now that I'd gotten away from work, Thomas was the thing I should focus on. In the kitchen, I poured milk into his plastic superheroes cup which he held in both hands as he guzzled down his milk, panting as he handed it back to me because clearly this was very hard work for him.

"Daddy is very strong," he said.

"Yes, he is."

"He chopped down nearly a whole tree." Thomas reached into the air, spreading his arms to emulate a large tree.

"A whole tree?"

"Well, a lot of branches."

I wasn't sure what Thomas was going on about, when the two of them had visited Baba and played Uno. Perhaps he was still slightly concussed.

"Did you have a good time with Daddy today?"

He nodded. "Can I show you how to build a blanket fort?"

"Sure, pumpkin."

This was one of Nick's famous tricks, and it worked beautifully. I had to hand it to him. He'd started proving himself with Thomas right away, kept him entertained, hadn't let him run around, and Thomas loved every minute of his 'Daddy time.' Both of them did.

I was glad I'd let Nick see Thomas after he got out of hospital. There'd been no point trying to deny him access when legally I didn't have a leg to stand on. And no money for lawyers either.

It had been hard. One of the hardest things I'd ever had to do.

My first thought hadn't even been a thought. It'd been fear of leaving Thomas alone with Nick, a wrenching in my gut, a stabbing in my heart. I'd have visions of Thomas hitting his head in the bath even though I hadn't been there. I'd see the doctor's face, lips moving, words coming out, but nothing making sense. And Thomas in the hospital bed unable to keep his eyes open.

I'd see all those things and at the same time, I knew I couldn't keep going that way. So I told myself to start letting go—of the apron strings in situations where I knew Thomas was safe, of my overprotective ways, and of Nick.

That tie was cut, severed, finished.

CHAPTER TWENTY

Nick

Beer wasn't bad, I told myself, as the first mouthful went down. In fact, it was pretty damned good. I was at The Swamp with Austin, but we were not having a repeat performance of last time. One beer and I was done.

As soon as Austin had arrived, he'd asked about Thomas and that showed the kind of person he was. The second thing he'd done was hand me a gift bag containing a Duplo police station, the perfect present for a little kid from an architect.

It warmed my heart to know he cared. The other guys too. Lachie and Cooper had been calling and had even stopped by to visit Lily with flowers after Thomas had first come home. More heartwarming stuff.

Austin sat opposite me at a corner table. "It wasn't your fault. Kids do stupid shit all the time."

The beer got caught in my throat. "Tell Lily that."

He drummed his fingers on the table. "I would if I thought she'd listen. It might take time, but she'll come around, Nick."

She wasn't standing between me and Thomas. She was letting me be a father. She'd always been dutiful when it came to things like that, but there wasn't even the smallest chink in her armor that might indicate she was coming around to me and her. Because there was no 'me and her.'

The weight of what I'd lost and what could've been pressed down on my shoulders.

Austin raised his eyebrows. "There's more to it, isn't there?"

I slid my glass down to the table. "There's always more."

Surprise shone in his eyes. "Hey, you and Lily… Did the two of you get back together?"

"Yep."

Eventually Austin said, "I didn't know."

"Not a lot of people did."

Though she'd never said it in as many words, Lily hadn't wanted our renewed relationship to become common knowledge. Another thing that'd been wrong, only I hadn't seen it sooner. Because if you were in a relationship, it *should* be known and not some dirty little secret.

Nothing we'd done had been dirty. And none of it was a mistake. No, a mistake was what I'd made with Thomas.

"But you're not together anymore?" Austin asked.

I shook my head.

He gave me a one-armed hug. "I'm sorry to hear that, Nick."

"I'm sorry too," I said, "about being an asshole the other day."

Austin held out his hand. "Don't worry about it. You've got other things to worry about."

I nodded. "Like the bar." It was the reason I asked him here.

He looked around the room, knocked back the rest of

his beer, and wandered across to the doorway leading to the band room. Leaving my glass on the table, I joined him. I gave him some space because he was thinking.

"Do you have a grand vision for this place?" he asked. "What kind of venue do you want it to be? Do you want to gut the interior and start from scratch, get something slick and contemporary?"

"Nah, that's not what I had in mind. I want it to be like it was, only better. I want to be true to the history of the place and create something where we can continue that tradition and build a new history. The best days of The Swamp aren't behind us. I want them to be ahead."

I meandered into the band room, memories of our early gigs coming back, the atmosphere of the place, the feeling that anything could happen and often did.

I kept going. "It'll be a place for locals and anyone who wants to hear good music. Somewhere that nurtures the local band scene but has standards and gives people what they want. We could have smaller bands during the week and the bigger names on the weekends to bring in the crowds."

"So the band room can stay?"

"Definitely."

"I'm glad you said that."

I spread my arms. "This'll be a bigger, better version of The Swamp. The New Swamp."

Austin nodded. "I like the way you want to maintain the integrity of the place."

Integrity? He'd said this seriously, but we looked at each other and laughed. The place was a dump, and we'd had stuff thrown at us on stage, seen guys throwing up outside, and all kinds of shit going on.

"Yep, integrity," I said.

Austin turned to face the bar. "I'd like to talk to your staff too to see how the set-up functions behind the bar, so we can build in any improvements and make sure they've got everything they need."

I snorted. "Good luck talking to Tara."

"Where is she today?"

"It's her day off."

We talked some more about the sound quality, which was shit, and access to the bar from the band room. Also shit.

Austin walked across to the bar, sat on a stool and kept looking around. He held a hand out to the bartender so she knew he didn't need a drink. I joined him and asked for a glass of water.

"Has your father been around to see the place?" he asked.

"No."

"I thought he might be interested since you've bought a business, you know, like you're moving into his world."

"You thought wrong."

Austin nodded but didn't say anything.

I'd thought the same as him, though. I'd hoped my dad might come by. I'd been searching for some common ground between us and had ached inside because all this time I'd been hoping for his approval. And I'd thought the bar might've been a good way of getting it.

It was hard to be honest, but the truth was that my father was part of the reason I'd bought the place. The little kid inside me had thought I could become the son he wanted me to be. Except that was never going to happen.

There was one thing I could thank him for, though. A

journalist had once asked me where a rich kid like me had found the drive to make it in the music industry. I'd resented the question because I knew the answer. My father. I had to prove to him I was a success.

So maybe it was time for me to be honest with him too.

Because I was done fucking around.

CHAPTER TWENTY-ONE

Lily

My son, the card king. He was addicted to Uno, and it was the best thing ever because it kept him occupied so he wasn't running around, at risk of bumping into things.

Sitting at the kitchen table, Baba threw her hands up in mock despair. "This child, he beats me every time."

Thomas grinned, swinging his legs under the table, feeling pleased with himself. Not surprisingly, he liked winning. Couldn't blame him.

"Maybe I should teach Dida too," he suggested. "So he doesn't miss out."

"That would be nice," my grandfather said.

His dementia came in waves, and today he seemed less blank than the last few times I'd seen him, so perhaps Thomas' idea was a good one.

"You'll have to go slow with Dida and take your time."

"Yes, Mommy."

My grandfather shuffled over to a kitchen drawer. "I have a better idea."

I started to worry because it was hard to tell what he might come up with, then relief washed over me as he passed across a deck of Italian cards to Thomas whose eyes glowed with delight.

"Ooh, look at these patterns. Look at this one."

Baba motioned for me to get up and join her just outside the door. It gave Thomas and his great grandfather some time together, and I could still keep an eye on them.

I couldn't help being overprotective, but I tried to balance it out. Like with Nick. I was trying.

I let out a long sigh. Somehow the men in my life never seemed to last. I'd lost my father when I was ten, so I'd been old enough to love him and then feel the hole in my heart. Then Nick had left me, and if I'd thought he'd come back to me, I was sadly mistaken. And I was losing Dida slowly bit by bit with his condition.

Baba nudged me. "Look at my big tree."

It was hard to miss the oak in the middle of the yard. Much better for me to think of something big and stable rather than the things I'd lost. Besides, Baba deserved my full attention.

"You're not going to tell me one of my uncles finally got around to pruning it for you?" I said.

"No, they're too lazy."

Baba was nothing if not blunt.

"Don't tell me you hired someone to do that for you," I said.

"Nick came by."

"I know, but what about the tree?"

"I told you. Nick came by."

"And pruned the tree for you?"

She nodded.

I clapped a hand over my mouth. Thomas had already told me this, but it'd seemed so far-fetched I'd thought the poor kid was still confused. Turned out I was the one who was confused, who'd underestimated Nick.

Something clutched at my gut: regret, remorse, a resurgence of feelings I shouldn't be having. Out of nowhere, tears started burning at the back of my eyes, tears that shouldn't even have been there. I bit my lip to hold them back. I told myself Nick wasn't worth it.

I lied to myself over and over again because we could have had something wonderful, and it was gone. I pretended I didn't care. Damn it, no wonder my stomach felt like it was being turned inside out.

Thomas shot past me, but I grabbed him before he could get far.

"No running, remember?" I said.

"Okay." He composed himself. "That's what Daddy said too. I'll just keep walking."

He made a big show of swinging his arms as he strode away. Baba opened her mouth to speak, but I got in first.

"This isn't me being overprotective. This is doctor's orders after his concussion."

"Yes, yes, I know." She played innocent though I had no doubt she was going to tell me I was overreacting. It was one of the reasons I loved her. The main reason was simpler. It was just because I did.

That was the thing about love. You didn't have a lot of control over it.

It could take over your heart until it was as much as you could do to keep breathing. It could hurt so much, you thought you wouldn't be able to make it. Like it did now.

Didn't matter what my mind said. My heart always came back to the same place. Nick.

CHAPTER TWENTY-TWO

Nick

Mom had gone to lunch with a group of ladies. She was always out lunching. Fine by me. It left me alone with my father to talk business because that was all we had, some final business, nothing more.

He leaned back in his chair in the living room, *his* chair, the best seat in the room that faced the television so that anyone on the couch had to crank their head. That said something about him, even if I hadn't realized it before.

He was cradling his post-lunch gin and tonic in his hand while I was so parched I gulped back a glass of water. I knew why my mouth was dry. Nerves. Better to get this over with.

I cleared my throat. "I told you about Thomas' concussion, and you haven't even called to see how he's doing."

My father shrugged. "You said he was fine."

"He is. That's beside the point. You're his grandfather. I thought you'd care. I though Mom might too."

"Don't be ridiculous. Of course we care. We've had a

lot going on, that's all."

"So you've been too busy even for a fucking phone call."

He slammed his glass on the side table, liquid sloshing out. "Don't talk to me that way."

"Sorry, is that too crude for your fragile sensibilities?"

My father was the least delicate man I knew. And if he thought he was better than me because he didn't swear, he was wrong, very wrong.

His eyes narrowed. "Have you got a bone to pick with me, son?"

A bone? More like a whole skeleton, something the size of a blue whale.

I leaned forward, arms resting on my thighs. "There are a few things I wanted to tell you."

"Any reason I should be interested?"

"Oh, I know you're not interested. And I don't care. You're missing out with Thomas. He's growing up so fast that those years will be gone if you don't make the most of them."

He shrugged. "All children grow up fast."

"He's a great kid, and you're so egotistical and self-centered you'll probably never even get to know him properly."

"Egotistical? That's rich coming from you."

I caught his gaze. "In part, I am what you made me."

"I don't think so." He sneered, looking down his nose at me. "I didn't make you a *rock star*."

He said the last two words as if he were talking about a killer or a drug dealer. I wasn't going to bother telling him I was a musician and songwriter. No point.

"Nah," I said. "I did that part myself. I came here to

tell you I don't care what you think."

His lips spread to a slow grin. "Ha! If you don't care, why even come? Your presence here just proves how much you care."

I wandered to the sideboard filled with family photos. There were a couple of photos of Thomas, and I was in a few family shots, but the bulk of the real estate was taken up by photos of my sister. Sophia's first steps, her prom, her graduation, her skiing vacations, her wedding, her honeymoon in the Bahamas.

A miracle happened. The rejection and pain I used to feel simply wasn't there anymore.

I turned to my father. "You don't get it. This was your chance to reach out. Or not reach out."

Confusion colored his face. "What are you talking about?"

"I'm done, Dad. I'm cleaning up my act. I'm going to refurbish the bar, and the band is cutting a new record which will be the best one yet. And I'm going to be the best father I can be."

"So what? Am I supposed to care about your grand statements?"

"Nope." I strode away, then stopped in the doorway. "I've got more important things to do too. I'm going to be with Thomas. You can call me any time you like. Don't think you can't."

I didn't bother listening to his remonstrations. I kept walking.

*   *   *

Another day, another blanket fort with the table in my apartment, and there was nowhere I'd rather be. Except for the bad back and the crick in my neck. Minor details.

The doorbell rang. Thomas looked ready to jump up, but I grabbed him before he hit his head on the underside of the table.

"That'll be Mommy." His eyes lit up. "I can show her how we built the police station in the fort and how the burglars are hiding under the cushion."

"Nice and easy does it."

As Thomas helped me out from under the table as if I were an old man, I wondered what the paparazzi would make of this if they could see it. Not to mention the headlines. *Rock Star Commandeers Duplo Police Station.* The headline they'd never print.

He took a couple of steps running when I called out, "Remember the speed walking I showed you."

A genius way of getting him to slow down, if I did say so myself. He speed walked to the door and waited for me to open it. I pulled the door open. The sight of Lily made my heart swell and sink at the same time because she was so close and yet so far.

I sucked in a deep breath. "I believe you need to look at the police station Thomas built."

I believe you need to stay. Because we can be so good together. Because you feel this too, Lily. The words I didn't dare say.

Thomas showed her the fort. She looked around the room and pointed to the coffee table. "I see you've been getting into the Play-Doh."

"Yep." I nodded. "It's kinda messy but it's a good, stationary game, no running around."

Lily laughed. A breakthrough.

Thomas rushed to the coffee table. "I can show you my Play-Doh too, Mommy."

She smoothed down his hair. "I think we need to get

going, honey."

Thomas turned to me. "Can I have a glass of water, please?"

"Sure thing." I motioned for him to join me. "This way."

Lily joined us in the kitchen while Thomas sipped cold water from his new Superman glass, making a production of it with a lot of sound effects and slurping. Lily leaned back against the countertop and looked around, a frown forming in her brow.

I spread my arms. "What?"

"Nothing," she said.

"I cleaned up."

"I can tell."

I held her gaze. "I've cleaned up a lot of things, Lily. I made sure there's milk and food in the fridge. There are some beers in there too, but I got rid of the other stuff, the bourbon and the vodka. I don't need it."

"You tipped it down the sink? Really?"

I shook my head. "I gave it to the young guys over the road because I thought they could make good use of it. You should've seen the looks on their faces. Free booze, they couldn't believe it. Now I'm their new best friend."

She nodded, put Thomas' empty glass in the sink, and turned away, her hands on his shoulders.

Sidling up close behind her, I whispered, "I'd like to be your best friend too, Lily."

She flinched, didn't say anything, then kept moving.

Thomas had already decided he wanted to leave his toys here for next time so there was nothing to pack up. I gave him a big hug at the door and a little piece broke off my heart.

I didn't want to say goodbye. I wanted him to stay with me. Lily too. Most of all, Lily.

"Bye, Nick," she said, opening the front door. "And thanks."

"You don't need to thank me. I'm his father." She'd already turned away, so I touched her arm. "I'm not giving up, Lily. I never give up."

Breathless, she looked into my eyes, but she wasn't mine. Not yet.

CHAPTER TWENTY-THREE

Lily

Nick walked through the door of the Silver Swallow, and my heart did a stutter step. How did he know I'd be here? Because not for a moment did I think he was here for the poetry and stories slam night.

Scanning the room, he spotted me and Amber at a table down the back and waved before heading to the bar. He got served instantly, of course, because that was the sort of power he had. Not over me, though.

"I wonder if he's getting us margaritas," Amber said.

"Amber!"

She shrugged. "What? He did last time. Just saying."

Sure enough, he wandered toward us, two margarita glasses in his hands. Swaggered more like it. The sight of him in those jeans shouldn't do this to me—shouldn't do anything at all—but it made me long for something I couldn't have.

He placed the drinks on the table. "Ladies."

"Ooh, thanks." Amber looked way too comfortable and not at all surprised to see Nick. "Can I have another photo, please, please. It'll make my friends even more jealous."

Which was probably why I didn't take social media so seriously. I posted a few pictures of myself and Thomas from time to time and checked out what my friends were doing, but I was under no illusions about the medium.

Amber had her phone at the ready as Nick put his arm around her and smiled. Clearly overjoyed, her smile took up her whole face.

He didn't sit beside her, instead walking to the other side of the table to slide onto the chair next to mine. I let out a long, slow sigh, the air between us charged, my stomach surging. This was beyond butterflies.

How could he do this to me? He wasn't the man I thought he was and yet… And yet, he was.

My insides melted just a little, enough to take the edge off, but he'd thrown me. That was the problem. He kept tossing me these curveballs by being such a wonderful father and cleaning up his act. He was like the Nick I'd fallen in love with, only better, more mature, more real. Something tugged inside my heart because it wasn't an act. It couldn't be.

I swallowed my doubts and forced myself to concentrate on the moment. I was here now. Surely, the simple act of having a conversation wasn't beyond me.

"I sent off my application for Frankston College." I hadn't told him earlier, not that I needed to but for some reason now I wanted to.

He raised his eyebrows. "Really?"

"They have a special late entry category and I figured if this doesn't work, there's always next year."

"It'll work, Lily. I'm behind you all the way."

I shrugged. "I'm not so sure. Between my job and Thomas, I don't know if I'll be able to juggle all my commitments."

"Maybe you can quit your job. That'd be the best thing."

Easier said than done. I could take money from Nick for Thomas, but I couldn't accept an allowance for myself. He wasn't my husband or partner, just the father of my child, and there was a big difference.

He must've seen the doubt in my eyes because he said, "Things have a way of working out if you let them."

I wished I could believe him. My heart twisted because of the things we'd done wrong, the mistakes we'd both made, because of the love swelling inside me. That was what made this so hard.

The emcee got up on stage. A distraction, thank goodness.

I sipped my drink. I'd almost forgotten about it. Amber peered at me over the top of her salt-rimmed glass because clearly her margarita was top of mind for her. A waitress delivered Nick a glass of water.

He started fidgeting as soon as the first act started, a serious young woman with a very long poem that I couldn't follow. Still, parts of it were pretty. We clapped at the end.

Nick leaned closer. "Why don't you drink your margarita?"

I took another sip. "I am."

The second person up was an unlikely candidate, a young guy with a buzz cut straight out of the navy who talked about missing his mom, his dog, and his girlfriend, in no particular order. Nick started drumming his fingers on the table, so I covered his hand and he stopped.

I let my fingers fall. This wasn't like him.

The emcee looked around the room. "Now we have a special guest."

Nick stood. My heart stuttered. What was going on?

"The next person up is…"

As he walked to the front, Nick signaled for the emcee to stop. I glanced across at Amber whose eyes were glued to the stage, looking as guilty as ever. I'd bet she knew Nick was coming tonight.

He stepped up onto the stage and adjusted the microphone stand to his height, having a quiet word and a bit of a chuckle with the emcee who then left him to it.

Turning to the audience, Nick shook back his long hair. "For those of you who don't know me, my name is Nick Steel and I play in The Merchants of Menace. I'm lucky enough to make my living doing something I love."

He paused and looked around, uncomfortable though he was used to being on stage. "I've been here once before, and it's kinda nice not being recognized. Or if I have been recognized, you're not making a big deal of it. Except for Amber. Hi, Amber."

Her face lit up as he gave her a big wave, but she didn't dare turn to look at me. I clenched my jaw and told myself this was nothing to do with me, just Nick getting some stage time.

"I write songs. I sing. I do a lot of things." He stepped back, covered his mouth, then composed himself. "I make mistakes. I'm human like the rest of you." He looked around, making eye contact with the audience. "I'm not a poet, but I'm going to give it a go tonight."

Then he held my gaze and swallowed me whole as he

pulled a piece of paper from his back pocket. I couldn't move, couldn't get any air, couldn't do anything as he spoke in that mellifluous voice of his.

A fragile ego
Always trying to please
Not seeing the light
So clear to me now
The yearning in my heart
So huge a man can barely take it
Suddenly so certain
That life is nothing without you
And love is not a shackle
The great realization
Loving you
Doesn't mean losing me
It is life

My heart melted in my chest, my insides molten, emotion surging inside me. A strange sound escaped me, a splutter. I swallowed back the fear coursing through me because I was scared the poem was about me and scared it wasn't.

I was sinking into my chair, through the floor, clawing at the table to stay upright. Nick was a drug, and he was the antidote. He was everything I'd ever wanted, and more.

The paper in his hands slipped to the floor. He stared at me from across the room, blue eyes blazing even from this distance. With love? Was that what was in his eyes?

He placed the mic on the stand as he had probably done hundreds of times before. He didn't take his eyes off me.

As Nick stepped off the stage, my breath caught in my throat. I didn't want to think about what was happening, and I wanted it more than anything in the world.

Only a few people stood on the floor between us. They made way as he strode toward my table, knocked over a chair that was in his way, and fumbled in his pocket to pull out a small box. Little sparks went off in my heart.

It happened in slow motion. He got down on one knee. I gasped. He opened the ring box, the only time he took his eyes off mine. Even in the dim light, the ring sparkled. I stopped breathing.

"Lily, will you marry me?"

A hand on my chest, I nodded.

He looked into my eyes and whispered, "I can't hear you."

"Yes." I could speak after all.

Rising to his feet, he slid his arms around me and picked me up. My heart was ready to burst as he spun me around, and the room filled with cheering.

It was nothing compared to the cheering in my heart, the joy that flooded me, the certainty that this was right.

Nick slid me down to the floor.

I still couldn't believe it. "You bought a ring."

"Couldn't propose without one."

"You planned this?"

He nodded. "The only bit I couldn't plan was your answer."

And he held me close.

CHAPTER TWENTY-FOUR

Lily

Sometimes the most ordinary things could be the most wonderful. Taking Thomas to the park. Planning our weekend because we knew we'd have this weekend together and then the next one after that. Kissing Thomas goodnight. Kissing Nick goodnight and good morning and everything in between.

Breakfast with Nick and Thomas was my favorite part of the day for that exact reason. It meant we had the whole day ahead of us, and I was with my beloved boys.

Thomas swung his legs under the table. "Can I help you write more songs today, Daddy?"

Our son was such a huge 'help' to Nick that he wouldn't get anything done if Thomas was around today, and he still had to work out a couple of songs with Lachie.

I jumped in quickly. "Maybe another day, pumpkin. In the morning, you can play while I do a few things around the house."

He gave me a look worthy of a teenager. "That sounds a bit boring."

"Or you can do the housework for me." He quieted

174

down after that, so I added, "Then we're going to Josh's house in the afternoon."

"Yay!"

A miracle, a complete transformation.

Like my life.

I'd be starting college in a few months. A dream come true. My dream. Sometimes I wondered what I would've studied if I'd gone straight to college from school, but there was no point worrying about that because I hadn't gone to college the first time around. I was going now, and I knew where this would take me.

I'd be the best teacher I could be, and I'd be able to do what was right for my family. I'd also have school vacations with Thomas which had always been part of my grand plan. I'd be able to quit my job too because Nick was behind me one hundred percent so I didn't have to worry about money anymore and that made my life a hundred times easier.

"Time to brush your teeth," I reminded Thomas when he'd finished eating.

He scooted off without complaining.

I took the dishes to the sink, the most mundane of chores. Then Nick came up behind me, his hands on my waist, lips on my neck, and 'mundane' suddenly meant nothing to me.

I arched my back. "I like it when you nuzzle."

"I like it when you take your clothes off, but we can't always get what we want when we want it," he whispered.

I turned around and gave him a playful whack on the chest. "Maybe you're the one who should walk around barefoot and pregnant in the kitchen."

"Hey, I have songs to write, gigs to play, platinum

albums to cut." He did a Tarzan impression. "You college student, me musician."

"This is right. We're right together." On tiptoes, I placed my lips on his. "Did I mention that I love you?"

"Well, what a coincidence because I love you too. Did I tell you I've got a real estate agent coming around later today for an evaluation?"

"No, but that's good."

He was tossing up whether to sell his apartment or rent it out. Apparently, the only thing he liked about it was the music room, and he was planning on building one of those at the back of our place.

Because that was what this was. Our place, our family, our lives together.

And life had never felt so good.

Keep reading for a sneak preview of Book Two...

ACKNOWLEDGMENTS

First of all, a big thanks to my very own rock star and in-house consultant, James.

Thanks very much to the people I interviewed, all experts in your particular fields and very patient with my dumb questions—Jenny Kim, Brooke Lundy, Scott Wilson, Brendan Murphy and Jo Taylor. Thanks heaps, guys!

And of course thanks to my fabulous critique partners, Claire, Lorraine, Juanita, Teena and Anna.

ABOUT THE AUTHOR

Susanna Rogers is the author of rock star romances for adults and kick butt books for young adults. Inspired by her very own in-house rock star and years of going to gigs, she penned the Mosh Series after writing and releasing several young adult novels. She's also a kickboxer and dreams of empowering girls and guys around the globe to believe in themselves, to take care and follow their own dreams. She has a soft spot for romantic suspense, also with kick butt heroines, so you never know what might be coming up next.

She would love to hear from you—susannarogers.com.

If you like her books, please post a review on Amazon or Goodreads. She'd like that a lot.

DOWN & DIRTY
MOSH BOOK 2

CHAPTER ONE

Austin

Coming home was supposed to be a beautiful thing but after being away for so long I wasn't sure where I belonged anymore.

Still, one thing was for certain. Being back in Frankston beat the hell out of back-to-back tours and being on the road constantly. Or in the private jet. Not that any of us actually owned our own aircraft but none of us was going to say no to hiring one and, hey, it was such a practical means of transport.

That was how crazy our lives had become. It didn't seem real. Sometimes it felt as if I'd walked into someone else's life by accident.

And now we were at The Swamp, which was like turning the clock back to the beginning, the first gigs, the grungy music, the dive bars. The place was a dump but at least it wasn't pretending to be something it wasn't, and the beer was cold. Or at least I hoped it was.

Such a relief to be able to hang back and gaze at the crowd instead of being the guy everyone was looking at on stage. How did Nick even know all these people? He probably didn't.

"Oh my god, you're Austin Murphy!"

So much for not being recognized. "Yep, that's me."

Two wide-eyed girls giggled and asked for a photo. It only took a moment to help them out and it made their day so I was happy to go along with it, but they looked so young that they made me feel ancient. Not that thirty was old. It was just the beginning, maybe a new beginning.

That decided it. I needed a drink so I edged my way closer to the bar. Didn't quite make it. The bartender handed across a cocktail, that was all she did, yet she looked like she'd been transported from a 1950s Hollywood film set, the starlet waiting to be discovered. How could I not have noticed her earlier?

It wasn't the red lipstick and blue eyes lined with black, or the jet black hair with the purple streak, or the polka dot shirt tied at the waist that had rockabilly written all over it that grabbed me. It was the confidence in her movements, the fire in her eyes, the personality in her face.

And maybe, just a little, it was those boobs in the push-up bra. My mouth dry, I swallowed. Yep, definitely the boobs.

Wiping the sweat from my forehead, I realized she was serving Nick and Lily. Giving Nick a serve too, by the look of it, which only made me like this woman more. Then she was onto the next customer, smiling, making eye contact, shaking up the next cocktail. She wasn't just a bartender. She looked like she owned the place, which was a lot more than I could say for Nick, who was most likely in full-on drinking mode.

Now I needed a beer more than ever but I had to get my shit together before I went up to the bar or I was going to look like a total jerk. Just two minutes, that was all I'd need.

Turning away, I tried not to stare. And failed.

Then Lachie came my way, gave me a fist bump. "Man, I love this place."

I glanced at the bar or, rather, the bartender. "I'm loving it too."

"Look at all this talent. We're surrounded by fans, girls, pretty young things who want us."

I held a hand out, as if pushing them away. "That's not for me."

Lachie made out like he was a party animal. And he was. But underneath, there was a big kid who'd insisted on coming back home so he could help take care of his dad. He had a huge heart even if he didn't want anyone to see it.

"And it's all free," he added. "Free beer, free booze, whatever we want."

"It's not free. Nick's paying."

He brushed it off and knocked back some more beer.

I'd been through this with him before. Nothing was free in this business. Anything the record company spent got charged back to us, as we'd found out early in the game. When we'd first started we were like little kids, excited about the limo greeting us at the airport, the bottles of Bolly, the huge parties the label put on, the hot shots who charged for the pleasure of their presence— until we realized we were paying for it all.

"Gotta make sure Nick has plenty to drink too," Lachie said. "Maybe even a little drinking competition."

I glanced at Lily through the crowd. "Give him a break."

"What? He's the one who's put on the party."

"All I'm saying is just let things take their own course. It's not like he needs any encouragement."

And neither do you. Suddenly I felt like a sad ass aging rock star. Yet another reason I didn't quite fit with the guys.

I glanced at the bartender and felt a surge of energy. That was more like it.

Lachie looked around, frowning. "What's this shit they're playing?"

I raised my eyebrows. "That 'shit' would be Elvis." He didn't say anything so I added, "From the Sun Sessions."

Definitely not Nick's choice of music. The other guys loved my bass playing, and they appreciated what I brought to the table, the way I could boogie over a shuffle all day long, but they weren't into rockabilly and old style rock 'n' roll the way I was.

Lachie leaned closer. "Can I get you a drink?"

"I'm good, thanks."

A small lie because I was getting that drink myself, and I'd already spent way too much time with Lachie when I had other things in mind. He was so drunk he probably hadn't seen me eying up the bartender. Probably just as well. Then he was off.

I didn't even know why I was talking to Lachie when I should be getting closer to the babe behind the bar. Only one thing stood between me and her, or maybe two things, Nick and Lily.

It would've been rude not to greet Nick. It was his bar, his party, and he was the one I was going to let down when he found out what was coming. My throat tight, I swallowed, trying to act like everything was fine.

I gave Lily a hug. She was a petite little thing, especially when she was next to Nick, and there was always something that made me feel for her, even if I couldn't work out what it was.

I asked about their son because he was a cute kid. Also I didn't think the other guys quite got what it meant to have a child of your own. Not that I did, but I tried to put myself in other people's shoes sometimes.

Like Nick, for instance. He wasn't the world's best partner to Lily, not her partner at all in fact, but he'd always done his bit as a father and he was overjoyed to be back with his boy. You could see it in his eyes.

I glanced at the bar, pretended I wasn't staring, and tried to look suave in case the bartender looked my way. She didn't. Somehow I ended up feeling more like a bumbling schoolboy than a famous musician. Not that 'famous' was important to me but that woman might be.

I turned to Nick. "I can't believe you bought The Swamp. Man, this brings back memories."

"Sure does," he said.

Problem was, his memories were completely different from mine even though we played the same gigs to the same crowds, most of them anyway. He and Lachie went back further than The Merchants. They'd always been tight. Meanwhile, Cooper had gone to school with them and was the best rock 'n' roll drummer around, in my humble opinion.

And then there was me. Even four years down the track, I was still the new guy.

I got that strange sensation of being alone in a room full of people, of being the odd one out, a feeling I got a lot despite the fact these guys were my friends and they were good people.

They might not be so friendly when they found out what was coming their way, though. It made my gut clench, made me feel like even more of an outsider. Still, I couldn't say anything tonight, as much as I wanted to get it over and done with.

I'd always got on well with Lily because in some ways she was older than the other guys in the band, not in years, but she'd had to grow up quickly after getting pregnant. Maybe that made her different.

Leaning over, I whispered in her ear, "Do you ever feel out of place?"

She chuckled. "All the time!"

I laughed too. Because it was better than crying. Besides, I reveled in the things that made me different, my individuality and my distinct tastes and experiences, even if they were the very things that singled me out.

Still smiling, Lily gazed longingly at Nick who wasn't even looking her way. That was when it hit me like a baseball bat, so clear I didn't know why I hadn't seen it before. She was still into him. Big time. Maybe even still in love.

Man, I felt for her because Nick's head was somewhere else. His dick had been a lot of other places too, not that I was much better. Until recently when I decided I'd had enough of all that rock star bullshit. Because that's exactly what it was. A load of crap.

I wished I could help Lily but this was so far out of my league it wasn't funny and I had enough problems of my own.

I told the two of them I'd join them in the band room, then turned to the bar and got a glimpse of that amazing bartender, a jolt rocketing through my whole body. And I mean, my *whole* body. I tried to shake it off and suck some air in.

Miss Rockabilly Bartender caught my eye as I leaned against the bar, acknowledged me with a nod, and kept serving her current customers. I had to admire her professional approach. In fact, there was a lot to admire as she leaned forward to listen to them place their order. It was getting kind of noisy in here, not necessarily a bad thing. Maybe I'd have to get close too so she could hear me.

She came over as soon as she was done with them. "What can I get you?"

"Beer, thanks."

"What kind?"

"What would you recommend?" Hopefully I sounded more like James Bond than Homer Simpson.

She stepped to one side so I could see behind her. "We've got a range of beers in the fridge and a couple on tap."

But I wasn't looking at the beer selection, my eyes glued to the fabulous figure in front of me. This woman was all curves. I swallowed, deciding I'd go for something on tap. It'd take longer.

I pointed to the beer tap. "What's this one?"

"That's our Frankston IPA made right here in town."

I smiled. "Pale ale. Gotta be good if it's local."

She placed her hand on the tap and started pouring. Her hands looked very soft for a barmaid, her arms smooth and pale. I had to stop myself from reaching out and touching to see if she was real.

I took the beer from her. "Are you from around

here?"

This was a big town, a city really, with a small rockabilly scene, only I hadn't seen her around, which seemed unusual.

"I'm not from Nevada." She tilted her head. "I'm from all over the place."

"Intriguing."

"Believe me, it's not as exciting as it sounds."

"Have you worked here long?"

"Longer than your friend has owned the place."

I opened my mouth to speak. Of course, she knew I played in the band with Nick.

"Everyone knows who you are," she added.

"Not everyone. Bet your grandmother doesn't know."

She shrugged one pretty shoulder. "She doesn't know much anymore. She passed away a couple of years ago."

"I'm sorry."

"You're right, though. She used to listen to Frank Sinatra and Pat Boone. On a good day she might stretch to Barry Manilow, nothing heavier than that."

I sipped my beer. "So you didn't get your taste from her?"

She tossed her head back. "What makes you think I'm not a Manilow fan?"

"Elvis was playing earlier. Now it's Johnny Cash. My guess is you chose the music for tonight because Nick sure as hell didn't."

She smiled, gazed at me with those mesmerizing blue eyes, gave me her full attention. I could have stayed like this all night. In fact, I was thinking she could hold a lot more than my attention. There was one body part of mine in particular that she could hold all night long.

I gulped back some beer so I could settle down a bit because I wasn't going to make a good impression acting like a randy teenager.

"You remind me of a song," she said.

"Really?"

"*One of these things.*"

"Can't say I've heard it."

She leaned closer so I got a glimpse of creamy cleavage. "You've seen Sesame Street, haven't you? You must know the song where they show three red balloons and one blue and you're supposed to identify the item that doesn't belong." She hummed the tune.

"And I'm the blue balloon?"

She gave a long, slow nod.

"Ha! You've got that right."

How amazing that she'd known me for all of five minutes and she'd nailed it. It made me feel there was hope after all. The other guys didn't get it, didn't know how it felt to be an outsider, to be part of something and never really quite there.

"Looks like your other friend needs a drink," she said.

Lachie was leaning across the bar. She excused herself and served him, getting back to work.

Meanwhile, I hadn't even gotten her name. What the hell was I thinking? I hung near the bar, hoping she'd come closer but some guy started tending bar near me instead while she was busy at the other end.

I wasn't done yet, though, nowhere near it.

Strange sounds started coming from the band room, loud thumps followed by whoops and laughter. I looked around. Lachie wasn't here anymore and Nick had said he was going to the band room. It was never good when those two got together, not when they were both tanked up.

I drummed my fingers on the bar. I should go in there and break it up, whatever the hell it was those two were up to, and then I'd feel like a granddad again. Letting out a long sigh, I got up.

I only made it as far as the doorway when I saw bits of broken furniture on the stage at the far end, parachuting ripped down from the ceiling. It had Nick and Lachie's name written all over it. This was exactly the sort of stupid thing they'd do when they were drunk.

Lachie was on stage, lifting a chair ready to smash it, Nick beside him. Miss Rockabilly was there too, giving him a big shove. Nick stumbled, looked like a little kid about to get told off by the kindergarten teacher.

I couldn't hear what she said but it must've been good because Lachie was doubled over with laughter while she ushered Nick from the stage. That was the thing with Nick. Sometimes he needed a monumental kick up the butt before he'd pay attention, not that she was humiliating him, just putting a stop to his antics.

Now that the commotion was over, she yelled, "Come on, guys, there's plenty of drinks at the bar."

I'm not sure what it was—the way she took control, her refusal to let anyone push her around, or maybe it was still down to those boobs busting out of that top—but that decided it for me.

The woman was a firecracker.

And I needed a little explosion in my life.